The Element of Love

An Elemental Romance

National Bestselling Author
Joi Miner

Contents

Synopsis

There's no place in politics for love... and no place for love in war...

Kai, the Water Prince, found himself having to give up his hopes of choosing the woman that his heart desired and marrying for the sake of peace. As the day drew near when he would be forced to choose a queen to rule the entire Realm by his side, the tension weighed heavily on him. He had three choices, all queens and with amazing potential in their own right, but that didn't put Kai's mind at ease that his right to his heart's desires were being compromised for the greater good.

Shanira, the Fire Princess, was hotheaded and entitled, certain beyond the shadow of a doubt that she was the best suitor for the new king. The pairing of their kingdoms' resources the only logical choice, she would stop at nothing to ensure that she was the one who was given the throne that she felt only she deserved.

Lurra, the Land Princess, had no interest in ruling the realm. Her love for another distracted her from what was happening in front of her nose. When she is forced to see that love had her judgment flawed, she quickly tapped into the royalty she was meant to be and devoted herself to her kingdom and its people. But it may have happened too late.

Makani, the Wind Princess, was light-hearted and fun-loving, and the idea of having the responsibility of the entire realm wasn't the least bit appealing to her. Add the fact that Kai, her potential suitor, was her twin brother Kari's best friend, and that made her even less interested. Going through life unbothered, she was struck with a love that couldn't be denied. A love that was bound to change her whole life.

In the Elemental Realm, to prevent the dangers of another Realm War, the rulers of the Wind, Land, Fire, and Water Kingdoms all came together on the terms of a treaty. Using their children as bargaining chips, may have done more damage than good. When egos come into play, everyone and everything, in the Elemental Realm *and* on Earth, may be at stake.

Dedication

To the woman who has taught me the difference between a political pairing and true love, thank you. I love you today, tomorrow, and always.

Chapter One

Serah Eve

It was a time of unrest in the Elemental Kingdom. The tension was heavy, and the Kingdoms were making their final preparations for Serah, the bright time, when the Orange Star outshone the moons and caused disruption in the balance of their Realm. Each Kingdom had to make provisions to protect itself, all but the Fire Kingdom, which thrived in this time because they so closely resembled the Orange Star.

The Land Kingdom had been in negotiations to ensure that they remained properly hydrated. Too much heat from the Orange Star would dry the land and cause it to crack open, along with its occupants, who were primarily composed of clay and stone. In return, the Land Kingdom provided wood, stone, and sand to protect the Water Kingdom from evaporation. The Wind Kingdom had a long-standing alliance with the Water Kingdom that allowed them to maintain their moisture and the ability to mist and move freely throughout the heat. These were necessary concerns and had kept the Royal Families locked in discussions for some time now. The Fire King presided over the discussions and offered suggestions, as his kind were well-versed in the Star, its dangers, and abilities.

Everyone was moving through their tasks and fear hung thick as fog. Beings were skittering to their respective corners of the Realm. The memories of the last Serah, sixty-five million Earth years before, and it leading to chaos, extinction of the Large Lizard, and near complete destruction of the Earth that the Realm governed, were on every tongue. Everyone knew that the slightest disagreement could lead to another war. So the discussions remaining amicable was paramount to the existence of all. The turmoil could even be felt on Earth, stirring up claims of Governmental climate control machines and other conspiracy theories because of the odd weather patterns, marine maelstrom, and tectonic plate shifts.

When the day ended, everyone rushed to their homes. The Realm, known for its parties following the completion of their tasks, was dead silent. An eerie silence draped every corner of the Realm. A silence that would remain until the Announcement Ceremony following the Courtship of the Three, when Water Prince Kai would court and choose one of the three Princesses and honor the Treaty through their nuptials. The weight of the Realm rested on this young Prince's shoulders.

****

Kai stared out of the window. His broad, dense frame sat solidly on the ledge of the windowsill. He wasn't himself. His eyes were puffy from lack of sleep. He'd been in a sullen mood. His pain draining down onto the Earth as unexpected rain showers. He hadn't even finger-combed his flowing clear tresses with Sand powder to give it his classic spiked look.

Danksha was his favorite time of the day. He loved to watch the dual moons rise, playing a cat and mouse game, their dim light casting varying shades of blue across the Elemental Realm. Normally, he'd rush to complete his chores, so he could sit and admire the beauty of it. But today, he had dragged through his tasks, setting the weather cycles haphazardly, missing his usual chill time with Kari that caused the waves to rise and fall. The Earth's oceans instead, rested and rippled in a somber calm. He'd dragged his feet to his room, leaving puddles all over the place.

Tonight was the last Danksha before the Serah. Kai had been told about this for as long as he could remember. The last Serah had caused uproar. The Elemental Realm had almost been destroyed. He was born during the upheaval, his mother Ava in hiding, while his father, Suavai, led the Water Warriors in battle against its three neighboring Kingdoms. He was the first of four other births that day, royalty in each Kingdom. Second was Shanira, a fireball and heir to the Fire Throne. Third, were Makani and her twin brother Kari, Fraternal twins, the spirited descendants of the Air Kingdom. And lastly, Lurra, the sound-minded heir to the Land Kingdom.

News of their births had caused a ceasefire, all of the kings wishing to live for their children, and not destroy the Elemental Realm that their offspring would inherit. A treaty had been formed, Kai being the foundation. It was his duty, Ava had explained, to marry one of the Princesses to maintain peace. Suavai had urged that he selected either Shanira or Lurra, because they were the most powerful, and trade with them could bolster the strength of the Water Kingdom. The pressure of it all, not having any real say in who he would spend his days with, stirred a tsunami in the pit of Kai's center. He was so wrapped up in his thoughts that he didn't even feel Kari blow past him.

Thinner than Kai, he was swifter on his feet. He was as light-hearted in frame as he was in nature. His head was bald. He had no time to bother with hair, it interrupted his fun. His eyes were wide and full of life and wonder. He rubbed his head, not liking the energy in the room.

"What's bugging you, Bruh?" Kari asked, startling Kai out of his thoughts.

"You know," Kai responded, giving his friend a frustrated look.

"Awww, come on, man," Kari grinned. "You've got your pick of three fine Princesses and you're upset about it?"

"Man, this is a lot of pressure. How would you feel if you had the weight of the Realm resting on your shoulders? One wrong choice, and we could be back at war again. And why aren't you bothered by the fact that one of those *fine Princesses* is your sister?"

"I feel you, Kai," Kari said, uncomfortably. He hated showing emotion, "and I'm not worried about Makani, because I would rather her end up with you than some other whack ass jackass."

Kari burst into laughter at Kai's side-eyed expression.

"Lighten up, my friend," Kari offered, halfway seriously. "It's your birth right. We all have a purpose. Yours just came with your pick of heiresses. If you want, I can test 'em out for you. All but Makani, of course."

Kai's saddened expression concerned his friend. They'd known each other since the treaty and Kari didn't know him to be the kind to worry about things like this. He knew there was something more to it. This was a heavy burden to bear and he'd been groomed for it for as long as they could both remember. But, the time actually coming when he would have to make a choice made it more reality than myth. More than a rumored tale that was told in passing.

"Have you met those Princesses?" Kai posed the question, although he knew the answer. They'd all grown up together.

"Yeah, man," Kari nodded. "You've definitely got some choosing to do. Shanira is so hotheaded. She doesn't think before she acts. Total abuse of power because she knows we'll clean up her mess. And Lurra, I don't even think she likes men. She's been Shanira's lapdog for so long, I think she'd rather be *her* pick than yours." He smiled at the thought.

Kai nudged him back out of his inappropriateness.

"And Makani is such a free-spirit, I wouldn't want to harness her..."

"You *can't* harness her," Kari corrected.

"Yeah and my parents don't want me to marry either Earth or Fire. Said that Wind didn't have enough political pull to make a partnership in the best interest of the Kingdom," Kai explained, not thinking before he spoke.

"Oh really," Kari gusted, angry that everyone thought the Kingdom that he would one day rule was the weakest of the four.

"Kari," Kai tried to explain. "That's not how *I feel*, that's how my parents feel, and you know how caught-up in tradition they all are."

"And how do you feel, Kai?" Kari asked, frustration moving him through the room, he was morphing into a tornado.

"How do I feel?" Kai asked, becoming uneasy with his friend's tirade. "You're my best friend, Kari. You and I do everything together. You're more integral to this Kingdom than Fire or Land would ever be. We do *everything* together."

This made Kari calm down. He settled in and looked at his friend. He'd heard all his life how weak and useless the other Kingdoms felt he was. But he knew better. Fire needed air to breathe. Earth needed Wind to carry its seeds so that it continued to blossom and flourish. Although it bothered him how his family was disrespected, his sister and Kai, the ones that mattered, made sure he knew where he belonged.

When he thought about this, he really began to feel for his friend. Soon, Kai would be caught up in the processes of being groomed for the throne. He would be married off to one of the Princesses and had no say in the matter. He wanted to help his friend. Say something to ease his mind. But he couldn't think of anything.

"How about I help you pick?" Kari finally asked, "I know you better than anyone, right?"

"Yeah," Kai answered.

"So, how about I chat them up. Then, I can watch your dates and even eavesdrop on them afterwards to see what they say," Kari offered, getting more and more excited about his own plan.

Kai smiled. He really liked the idea of having an extra hand in making such a heavy decision.

"But," he paused, "won't you be biased towards Makani?"

"Makani can stand her own ground. She's my *big* sister, remember, she beat me out," Kari laughed at the thought. "And," he added, "she's not thrilled at the thought of having to spend time with her little brother's stupid friend."

They both laughed and planned to meet later to plan out the details. This eased Kai's mind, just a little. He sat, enjoying the remainder of Danksha, knowing that he had a true ally in Kari.

Chapter Two

Courtships

The Palace had been prepared for Serah, heavy boards placed against the walls and windows so that the heat from the Orange Star didn't weaken and evaporate its occupants. It maintained the darkness, so Kai couldn't tell that the Orange Star had risen. He didn't remember it, but at some point he had fallen asleep. He had lost his form and had to recompose himself. The bustle of the servants rambling around outside his door, indicated that he had been asleep well into Serah.

Heavy knocks on the door told Kai that it was time. The Dolphins swam in to prepare him for his first courtship. He felt like a Mermaid being prepared for a burlesque show. Their incessant chatter didn't bother him, because it was being drowned out by the thoughts in his head. Shanira was spoiled and self-centered. She would probably spend the entire time talking about herself. Her arrogance knew no bounds. She was beautiful, and she knew it. She wanted to make sure that everyone else in the Realm knew it, as well. And she had a terrible temper. If things didn't go her way, she was liable to scorch entire lands.

When the dolphins took their leave, Ava entered with a broad smile on her face. Looking at her son in admiration, she liked the regal look that the dolphin stylists that she'd hired gave him. It was more mature than usual. His hair, that was usually spiked stiff, was cornrowed back and flowing down past his shoulders. His seaweed and starfish cape, hung around his shoulders, to the floor, revealing his bare chest. Koi was masterfully encased and swimming through his chest and torso. And his seafoam slacks were slim-fit, and dyed bronze, accentuating his seashell sneakers. She chuckled at the fact that, even when dressed for the ball, he refused to wear uncomfortable shoes. He looked like royalty.

"You look quite handsome this evening, Prince Kai," she complimented.

"Thanks," he responded halfheartedly.

"Not excited about your date with Miss Hot and Heavy?" she asked, her disdain for Shanira apparent. She was quite popular amongst the dignitaries and was not the kind of mate she wanted for her son.

"Not at all," Kai admitted. He could always be more honest with his mother than he could with his dad. Even though he'd married for love, the war had frightened him and made him more concerned with the treaty than matters of his son's heart.

"Just go out and try to have fun, son. You still have some say in who you will marry," she soothed.

"*Some* say, but not much," Kai pointed out, slamming his hand against his knee, causing thunder to clap. "I don't even know what I'm going for. Fire and Water don't mix."

"Calm yourself, Kai," Ava offered. "Go out and do your duty, and when it's over, we'll have kelp and listen to the Whale Orchestra."

This made him smile. She knew just how to make him feel better. He decided to do what he needed to do in order to protect his mother and the Kingdom whose throne he was set to inherit. Maybe Shanira would be on her best behavior. Kai chuckled a bit at the thought.

Soon after his mother left, the doors to his room burst open. Kari sauntered in looking quite dapper. He was wearing a Papier-mâché tuxedo, accessorized with wind chimes that drifted with every wispy motion. His currents moved through him more peacefully than Kai had ever seen, unless Kari was in slumber, and he drifted around on the drafts of his own confidence, his feet never touching the ground.

The Courtships were meant to be kicked off with a ball, and all royalty would be there. Kai closed the doors with a puff and a loud bang. Leaning up against the wall, he took full inventory of his friend.

"We are some handsome men, you know that?" Kari stated matter-of-factly.

"Yeah, we are," Kai confirmed, happy that his friend would be there with him during the ball and watching his Courtship afterwards. "You know you gone have to take the chimes off if you're gonna be incognito on your stealth mission."

"Alright, so I'll chat up Shanira first. You know she lives for attention."

"Especially yours," Kai interjected, referencing the way that she beamed anytime that she was in Kari's presence.

"Fire and Air, my friend," Kari stated, not flattered by the thought of that nutcase being interested in him. "You getting jealous?"

"Jealous of what?" Kai asked, realizing how his reaction could have been interpreted as such.

"Thought I heard a hint of it in your voice just then, my boy," Kari teased. "You know I've got a soft spot for mermaids. I wouldn't look twice at Shanira."

"I know," Kai stated, getting back to business. "So, you'll do the research and let me know, over dinner, what your pre-evaluation shows. Then, we'll compare all notes after dinner."

"Sounds like a plan," Kari confirmed. "See you in the meat market," he joked.

He exited the room much more suavely than he'd come. Leaving his friend to prepare for the night that lie ahead.

Bmmmp-bmmp-baaaaaannnnnnnppppp!

The horse fish horns blew, and Kai blew out a hard breath. *It's time*, he coached himself, opening the door to his quarters and walking out, climbing onto the seahorse drawn carriage that would lead him into the ballroom.

"Announcing Prince Kai of the Water Kingdom! Savior of the Elemental Realllllmmmmmm!" the announcer yelled, and everyone cheered loudly as the carriage entered the room. Kai was seated comfortably on the cushioned seats and was rolled into the expansive space once the announcer called attention to him, the man of the hour.

He was escorted, by a parade led by the symphony of trumpeting horse fish and taken to the seat beside his mother and Kari at the table. They exchanged notes, quietly, over their meal. Across the room sat the Princesses and parents.

Shanira was making eyes at Kari, beaming across the room in all of her glowing glory. She was adorned in a sheer fireproof gown, showing her greatest asset, her warmth. Her kind were at their strongest during Serah, and it showed. She flashed him a blinding smile that he met with a mild-mannered grin, and a head nod.

Diverting his eyes, they landed on Lurra, who looked very uncomfortable in her dressing. She was more inclined to wear bark and soil than the floral ensemble her parents had squeezed her into for the ball. She even had butterflies fluttering in her hair, and a bird's nest crown that sat atop her head and looked like it itched. Trying not to chuckle, he knew the feeling of discomfort that she felt, and kind of felt for her— and himself.

Taking a moment to compose himself, he looked further down the table and felt like all the air was sucked out of him. Kai was speechless when he laid eyes on Makani. Normally, as flighty as her brother, she looked poised in her formed self. Her soft features were highlighted with a golden pollen over her eyes and on her cheeks. Her dress showed the curves of her slim frame that he'd never taken notice of before. It was made of daffodils, the petals of some drifting off into the air that surrounded her. Kai grasped one in his hand, making a wish before blowing it back in her direction. She was breathtaking and a breath of fresh air at the same time. He tried not to stare but it was almost impossible. And it was apparent that she'd noticed him, too. They kept exchanging coy glances across the table over dinner.

During the ball, Kari and Kai danced with the Princesses to the sounds of the Anglers, featuring the Sea-famous Bobbie Blowfish on the Charonia, Oliver Octopus on the tentacles, and the Cris Crustacean on the keys. Each Princess was owed one dance, to see if a spark could be lit. The irony of it being that the first dance was owed to Shanira.

Kai found himself having to keep Shanira's attention while they danced. Her eyes kept drifting to Kari, who was chatting his sister up and dipping her in a playful, brotherly manner. Not that he was complaining, because he couldn't keep his focus off of Makani. So at least their focus was aimed in the same direction. But Kai knew that he had to do his due diligence, so he did his best to properly entertain her. When she wasn't staring at his best friend with hunger in her eyes, she was talking about herself.

"I know this is just a formality, so I'm going to allow you to entertain the other two but we both know that our union would be the best political decision that your kind has ever made."

"My kind, huh?" Kai asked, his frame rippling and the steam rising more quickly than before at the union of their touch.

"I mean, no offense, but yeah. And, look at me," she said, stepping back slightly so that he could see her in all her fiery glory. "Who wouldn't want to be with me?"

"I know a couple who wouldn't," Kai said under his breath, but she heard it.

"What did you say?" she asked, her glow shifting from yellow to a red-orange that everyone in the room knew too well. Kai didn't rescind his statement because he meant exactly what he'd said. Her hair licked straight upward like her finger had been stuck in a socket. And everything seemed to stop, even time. But, Kai was glad to realize that it was just the end of the song. He couldn't have been more grateful, because he would've hated to start a war by taking her temp down a couple of levels. He would've put her out if he needed to and been on the front lines of the rebellion against this mockery of a processional they called a Courtship.

Clapping when the song ended, he bowed to Shanira, but instead of curtseying, like a lady would, she gave him a glaring wink, letting him know that things were far from over. He shrugged, and met eyes with Kari, whose laughter was dancing in his eyes.

Walking across the room, Kai extended his hand to Lurra, pulling her from the corner she'd been holding up, and leading her to the center of the floor. He and Lurra fought the entire song for the lead. At one point, she stomped his seashell-toes so hard that she chipped the tip of one of them.

"I'm sorry," she apologized for what felt like the hundredth time. "I feel like a fish outta water," she said, her hand snatching from his in their waltz and covering her mouth. "Oh goodness, I'm—"

"Sorry," he finished for her, leaning in close to her ear so that she could hear what he had to say next. "It's fine. Relax. I hate this shit just as much as you do. And as soon as we get out of here, you can take that ridiculous nest off your head. I bet it's itchy, isn't it?"

"Yessss," she hissed, in a whisper, excitement in her voice. "I want to pat my weave so bad, but my mother would kill me. I don't understand the pomp and circumstance of all of this. Why can't they let us love who we love?"

There was a sadness in her tone that made me pull back and look into her face. Following her eyes, I saw that she was staring at Shanira longingly, confirming

Kari's statement from the night before. She was in love with her, and Shanira was either oblivious to that fact, or aware and using it to her advantage.

"There are some things that are just our duty," Kai stated to Lurra, quoting his father Suavai's words to him every year since he could comprehend them.

"Yes, but we didn't ask to be birthed into this. Why do we have to clean up the mess that they made before we were even a conception in their minds and hearts?"

"That is the million-dollar question," Kai said with a smile, a level of understanding and respect growing between them that neither of them expected. The song ended, and Kai kissed the back of Lurra's left hand before releasing it. When they both looked down, a bud had sprouted, blossoming into a rose. Blushing, she curtseyed as best she could before returning to the shadows of the corner on the ballroom she'd claimed as her own.

Kai's eyes surveyed the room looking for Makani. When he couldn't find her, he smiled at his mother at the table before walking over to her.

"May I have this dance?" he asked, more to Suavai that to Ava.

"Of course," Suavai said with a smile. He loved the relationship his wife and son shared. She was the flow to his ebb, less stern and with far less pressure. She allowed Kai to be much more fluid than he did, and he knew that his son not only needed, but appreciated that balance.

"Shall we?" Kai extended his hooked arm for his mother to take.

They drifted, effortlessly to the dance floor, and Kai didn't notice Ava give the conductor a head nod. When the music picked up with more tempo, Kai's smile couldn't be hidden, as they started playing a Hip-Hop rendition of his favorite song, "Baby Shark". Kai and Ava had spent many silly nights learning the choreography to the song, and showed their skills together on the floor, giving all of the Elemental Royalty and Council a show. Soon, everyone was joining in, and the ballroom floor looked like a flash mob. Laughter filled the air, and what was once a stuffy environment turned into a fun party with all in attendance having a ball. A few line dances later, Kai was exhausted, and Ava's shark tooth stiletto heels had her feet aching.

"I'm going to step out for a moment," Kai whispered into his mother's ear, kissing her cheek before returning her to his father's care, like the gentleman they'd raised him to be.

"Have fun?" Suavai asked, rippling with laughter.

"Yes, but I'm going to need some jellyfish shock therapy to bring my feet back to life," Ava teased, kissing her husband on the lips lovingly.

"I would catch every jellyfish in the Kingdom with my bare hands to awaken the feeling in those beautiful toes. You know tickling them is one of my favorite things to do," Suavai flirted, cupping Ava's cheek and pulling her leg into his lap, removing her shoe and massaging the sole of her left foot.

"I know," Ava said with an eyeroll of fake annoyance. The way that she blushed showed that her husband could still make her gush with just his words or a touch. Kai took in their interaction. The way they loved one another, regardless of who may have been watching. He wished to have that for himself, but that wasn't his fate, and that made him envious of them in that moment. The thought of a love so effortless took his mind back to Makani, making him survey the room for her again. But she was nowhere in sight.

He stepped out of the room in order to take a break from all the dancing and feigned pleasantries, leaning up against the wall to catch his breath. Hearing laughter and voices down the hallway, Kai shook his head and chuckled at Kari and Makani, playing hacky sack with a flounder. *Leave it to these two to not take something so serious seriously.*

"Y'all missing out on the fun," he said, scaring Makani and making her drop the flounder onto the floor. More of the dandelions flutter free from her dress.

"The fun's wherever we are, so maybe it's *you* who is truly missing out," she offered, making Kari laugh and fold his arms against his chest. He gave Kai a look as if to say, 'I told you so,' and Kai could do nothing but laugh because he could tell that Makani could, indeed, take care of herself. She was just as quick on her feet as her twin brother.

"Well, what do you say you and I take the fun back to this dancefloor, before the entire Realm explodes with whispers and rumors," Kai offered, and she shrugged nonchalantly, leading the way back into the ballroom.

Kari patted Kai on the back, because he knew his sister, and was sure that his best friend was about to have her hands full. Their chemistry was crazy, however, and even Kai could see it. He just hoped that Kai and Makani didn't get in their own way. Kai liked the playfulness of the banter, but the closer he got to the doors of the ballroom, the more the reality set in that there would have to be more to their connection than banter in order for him to justify his choice of the Princess of what was considered the least useful and influential kingdom in the realm as his mate.

He met Makani in the center of the dancefloor, taking her into his arms, and chill rushing through him. As they began to dance, their movements resembled that of the tides, easing up onto the beaches on Earth. With Makani, it was effortless, like when he chilled with Kari, but better. He had never given her a second glance, because of the treaty expectations and the fact that he was so close to his brother. But tonight, he saw her as the queenly being that she truly was.

They danced several songs, getting lost in one another, and completely losing track of time. At the end of the fourth song, while they stood lost in one another's eyes, Kai felt a gentle tap on his shoulder. Snapping to, he looked into the face of his father, who looked like he hated to be the bearer of bad news.

"It's time. Shanira is waiting for you," Suavai told his son, realizing for the first time the weight of the burden he'd placed on his son's shoulders. At the time, the treaty made sense, but now, he wasn't so sure.

Kai almost had to be pried away from her to be taken to the carriage awaiting him and Shanira.

"Don't worry. I'll be right here when you get back," Makani promised, trying to put on a brave face, and hide the fact that she was unhappy to have to share Kai with anyone else.

Chapter Three

Playing with Fire

When Suavai led Kai out of the ballroom, Kari was chatting up a mermaid. Kai hoped he wouldn't get caught up and forget their plan. He could be so scatterbrained sometimes. The shift of the crowd following Kai and Suavai to the outside of the ballroom was enough to get his attention.

"I thought you weren't coming," Shanira said, looking at Kai skeptically.

"And where would I be able to go and defy my destiny without the guilt of the destruction of our Realm and Earth choking me out of my sleep at night?" he asked sarcastically, dreading this courtship already.

"You act as if you would regret choosing me. But you have to realize that I'm giving up on a chance at real love to be with you, too. So, you're not doing me any favors, Kai. We're all in the same boat, so we might as well row this shit to shore."

Kai couldn't help himself, he found her last statement humorous. "What do you know about boats and water, Shanira, other than using the rows and boat materials to heighten your fire?"

"I know everything about you, Kai. What kind of mate and partner would I be if I didn't?" Shanira asked the rhetorical question.

Kai just nodded when he heard the seahorses whinny, alerting them that the carriage was about to head out to their date location. He looked out of the window to the carriage to see Makani standing at the door of the ballroom, Ava's hand wrapped soothingly around her shoulders. Sighing, he blew out a breath, deciding to make the best of his current situation.

The carriage took them to the far side of the Kingdom. The ride was silent and awkward, Kai's thoughts consumed with Makani, and Shanira unsure of why all of this was necessary when she already knew that she had the courtship in the bag. She eyed Kai, wondering if she could ever mate with him to bring forth a descendant. Wondering if they would only have a political marriage or if they could learn to love one another.

She had to admit he was handsome. And his confidence was intimidating. He, unlike most others in the Realm, knew that he was just as powerful as she was. But unlike her, he didn't flaunt his power. He was calm and something about him made her want to tone herself down. She wanted to explore it more, but only if she was certain that she would be his pick. *How does he have me doubting myself?* She questioned herself, realizing that her confidence was dimming more and more by the moment in the presence of this chill prince. *Maybe it's his mist that's causing me to simmer down. I can't let my weakness be shown*, she coached herself.

The carriage stopped, bringing both of them back to their surroundings. There was a layout of refreshments and protective gear so that Kai could take her Humpback whale riding.

"Sushi? Really?" Shanira snapped, looking at the food that was laid out.

It wasn't until she felt eyes on her and saw Kai's eyes on her, that she realized she'd spoken her thoughts aloud. She flashed him the million-watt smile that always got her out of trouble and couldn't help but admire the way that her light glistened against his surface. It was enchanting, and Kai was growing on her more and more by the moment. When her eyes traveled from his chiseled, marine-filled chest, she saw a disdain in his eyes that let her know he wasn't going to fall for her charms.

"Listen, I'm sorry. I just... raw fish isn't my thing," she tried to explain, shocking herself with her apology.

"But it's *mine*. Both our kingdoms would merge *if* we do marry. How do you think that's going to work if you're not willing to compromise and combine my preferences and yours?" he posed a real question.

Shanira hadn't thought about that. She hadn't missed the way he'd stressed the word "if" when he spoke of them marrying. She really thought that it would all be about her. She *was* the princess of the most powerful kingdom in the realm after all. It had *always* been all about her, and she didn't know if she liked the thought of that changing for the sake of the treaty. *I could always just take over the whole realm. No other kingdom holds a candle to us*, she laughed lightly at the pun. *I know Daddy would go to war for me, with a little persuasion.*

Shanira decided that to be her final ace in the hole. If Kai was stupid enough to choose anyone but her, she would take the entire realm and make him pay— with his life. And the Fire Kingdom would rule, like they should have from the jump. When she came back from her thoughts, Kai was staring at her with a concerned look on his face.

"You ok?" he asked, wondering what had her so consumed.

"Yes, and you're correct. I can't be selfish all my life. Even though being selfish isn't such a bad way to be," she tried to joke, but he didn't find it funny at all.

"It's a terrible way to be when you have to think of entire kingdoms, a realm, and Earth relying on you."

Tsk! She sucked her teeth, tired of him chastising her. "This is supposed to be a date, Kai. Are you going to spend the entire time together fussing at me?"

"Are you gonna make me?" he answered her question with a question. Raising his eyebrow, he could see that she had to *think* about the answer to the question, and that was too funny to him. Busting into laughter and Shanira joined in, breaking the awkward tension between them.

Kai made their plates, and Shanira watched him curiously. She never would've thought that the Prince of the Water Kingdom would be serving her a meal. It was sweet, but she couldn't see herself returning the favor. He solidified himself, his body now hard as the ocean floor, to hide his digestion. His flesh took on a scaly tone that reflected different shades of greens, blues, and purples depending where the light from her glow landed. He picked up an octopus roll and tossed it into his mouth, his sharp, shark-like teeth tearing into the flesh.

Shanira had to say this was one of the most unappealing things about him, but even that was tolerable. She touched the sushi with her fingertip, cooking it, and smiled at her own quick thinking. Turning her own temperature down to a smolder, she bit into the delicacy and had to admit that it wasn't bad. It wasn't cedar and bamboo with a Cajun cream sauce, but it was still good.

"Can you cook?" Kai asked, making Shanira ball up her face. She shook her head no. "Clean?" Another head shake. "Well, what can you do?" he asked, and she seemed insulted by the question.

"Can you cook or clean, Kai?" she asked, countering him, disgust in her tone.

"As a matter of fact, I can. My mother believes in equality, ebb and flow. She has taught me to care for myself and my mate properly. I couldn't imagine being someone that expected all these things be done for me all the time."

"But you have servants," Shanira pointed out, thinking that she had just caught him in a lie.

"We do, and they do their part to help keep the palace in order. However, I don't mind pitching in. I make my own bed and clean up after myself. I had chores coming up. My parents believe that a great leader knows every aspect of the people and place that they're leading. I have spent time with all of the creatures of my kingdom, volunteer, and have worked with every level of sea beast from krill to shark, merfolk to anemone."

"Ewww," Shanira belted out. At first, Kai thought she was referring to the kelp wrapped shrimp with Beluga caviar on top. But then he realized that she was enjoying the food and was repulsed by his pride in manual labor and community acts.

"So, the thought of being a part of the community that you rule bothers you?" Kai asked, shaking his head. He was ready for their date to be over in that moment. There was no way that he would ever be with someone like Shanira. If she was trying to change and improve, then maybe. But he knew that she wasn't trying to change her way of life, and most importantly, her way of thinking.

"Of course it does," she said like he was stupid. "I'm a *Princess*," she said, taking a sip of the Squid Ink wine that Kai poured for them both while he listened intently, searching for some kind of logic in her explanation.

"And I'm a Prince, so make it make sense."

"Listen Kai, you wouldn't understand because you don't know what it means to rule over the most powerful kingdom in the realm. You may *have* to learn to do all these things, but I don't. I know my place and my worth. You could learn something from me. I mean, I'm doing you a favor by even dressing up and agreeing to come out with you."

"You're doing *me* a favor?"

"Yes," she said with another sip of her Squid Ink wine. "We all know that, you beat Kari in being the "chosen one" for the treaty because of a sand dollar toss. If Makani hadn't come out first, I would be with him right now, instead of you," she used air quotes with the words 'chosen one' before taking more sushi into her mouth, chewing carefully before she completed her rant. "If we chose, ya know, if this little courtship race didn't exist or didn't go the way that we desired, the Fire Kingdom could destroy the Water and Land Kingdoms with little effort."

Shanira looked at Kai to make sure that he understood what she was saying. And she could tell by his tightened jaw that he understood completely. She was beginning to rub him the wrong way, but he was going to remain the gentleman that his mother raised him to be, despite her being the diva that she was known for being.

Sitting in silence, Kai finished his meal, and listened to Shanira continue on her tangent. Shanira went on and on about herself, and the many uses of her Kingdom's resources. She raved about how much UV light is traded for, and it being the most powerful form of currency in the realm. How integral heat was to Earth and how, without them, the planet would surely perish. How they could destroy the Land and Water Kingdoms and only kept them around because they were useful. "The only Kingdom that equals our power is Wind," she concluded with a heavy sigh, staring off into space in a way that made her true interest known.

Kai found himself rolling his eyes and thinking that she was so self-involved that she didn't realize that she was being insulting. But the more he listened to her, the more he realized that she could care less if she was insulting him. And things only went from bad to worse.

When they finished eating, well, she finished eating, because he'd lost his appetite, he got up and made his way to the changing area. There were two wooden partitions erected for them to change from their formal clothes and into the protective gear for the second portion of their date. She argued with him, not wanting to put on her protective gear.

"I have no interest in riding a whale and don't want to risk getting wet," she whined, "do you know what happens when you mix fire and water?"

"Shanira, put on the suit," Kai requested, attempting to remain calm, "let's go on this date and get it over with," he coaxed.

"No," she stated firmly, being a complete brat, "we both know that you are going to choose me. Spending time with those other *losers* is just a formality. And we'll marry and maintain the alliance, but I have no interest in being with you in any way intimately. I'll give you a single heir. We will remain in our respective Kingdoms, and make appearances, take trips, to keep up this rouse."

Kai stared at her, dumbfounded. He thought she had shown just how spoiled she was, but she kept leveling up on him. She became less and less attractive the more she spoke. There was no way that he would choose a pompous being. The air current shifted overhead and he could tell that Kari had been watching this entire scene. There was no doubt he was enjoying himself. Kai couldn't wait until this date was over. He had stopped listening to Shanira, everything she said now resembling the annoying, pointless chatter of the dolphins.

His mind drifted back to Makani. There had definitely been a spark there. He loved how easily everything flowed with them and was eager to see how their date would go. He smirked at the thought of there being a spark between Wind and Water, and no spark with the future Fire Queen. His smirk morphed into a smile at the thought of putting Shanira out. But he knew that such an act would lead to war.

"Ok... ok, that smile lets me know that you're finally coming around," Shanira grinned, arrogantly assuming that she was the motivation for the smile on his face. "Now, you will pay us a dowry, if your kingdom cannot afford it, we'll set payment arrangements and have a long engagement until it's paid in full," Shanira continued telling him what he was going to do *for her.*

"Shanira..." Kai snapped, his voice clapping forth like waves in the brewing of a storm. The sound startled her into silence and she stared at him, not knowing if she should be turned on or upset by his tone. "SHUT THE HELL UP!"

Something was ignited inside of her with the way he had just spoken to her. But it wasn't the fury that she was accustomed to, or what he expected. He planned to have to put her out and deal with the consequences later.

"Ooooh," she said, stepping into his space, making him change back to his fluid form so that he could be prepared for whatever was to come. "I like that."

Touching his chest with her blazing hand, the steam rose from his body, sending bubbles to his lower region. He looked at Shanira, thinking that she *was* beautiful, and he hadn't had any trysts in three months, in preparation for the Courtships. And his last encounter was with a stingray that just laid there like a barnacle on the back of a whale. He could have rocked his own boat for the effort that she put in.

Feeling the bubbles multiplying, he realized that Shanira's hand was traveling lower and lower by the second. *She's not even willing to let me take control in coitus, Kai* thought, frustrated. Stepping back, he shook his head. That seemed to be the theme of the courtship with her.

"That's not very ladylike, Shanira," he stated, making her suck her teeth and fold her arms.

"The thoughts you're having aren't very gentlemanly, either, Kai. Why are you acting like you don't want to fuse with me and make some precipitation!"

"Naw, I'll pass," Kai grunted, stepping further away from Shanira so that he could lower his own temperature. He had to admit that he was curious, but he didn't want to send any mixed signals when she was already so certain that they were going to be together. "There's plenty of time for all of that *if* we marry. I don't want to send you any mixed signals."

"There are no signals to mix, Kai. But have it your way," she said, blowing him a fiery kiss. "Your loss."

Kai saw the carriage approaching and it was the happiest he'd been since this courtship started. This had been the longest hour that he'd ever had in his life, and it frustrated him that they hadn't done anything but eat. Kai was convinced of two things by the end of their date. One being that Shanira loved the sound of her own voice. And the second, that he was *not* going to choose her as his life mate, contrary to her belief.

The carriage driver hopped out of his seat, opening the door for them. Extending his hand, Kai helped Shanira into the carriage, and she rested her head on his shoulder. He didn't push her away, just froze that part of himself into a glacier to withstand the heat that she was emitting. He knew that she was hoping that the crowd that had seen them out was going to be waiting anxiously for their return. She wanted to give the impression that they'd made a love connection. Kai wasn't a fan of false impressions, but he wasn't going to embarrass her, either.

The ride to the Fire Palace seemed to take forever. The sat in silence. Kai didn't want to chance her starting up again. He didn't think he could stand much more from her and remain cordial. He'd never seen such a vain creature. Mermaids weren't even that bad. He couldn't be happier to see her home come into view. When he saw what seemed like the entire Fire Kingdom awaiting their arrival, lining the streets and cheering them on as they entered the Palace walls, he almost pushed Shanira off of him. But he would let her make it a little while longer.

The closer they came to the Fire Palace; the more excited Kai became. He was ready to get home, lose form, and cuddle up with his mother to munch on kelp and listen to the Whale Orchestra. When the carriage eased to a stop, Kai waited for the driver to open the door, and stepped out first. Extending his hand once again, he assisted Shanira with her exit, and looked down at her. She was beautiful indeed, but she was so empty on the inside that her exterior wasn't appealing to him anymore.

"Thank you for tonight," Kai offered, courteously, leading her to her quarters. When they reached the door, he could tell that Shanira was expecting more than a thank you.

"Spend the night with me?" she asked, showing her vulnerability for the first time all night.

He knew she had weaknesses, and he knew she knew that, too. That inside she was a scared soul, wanting to be catered to, coddled, and taken care of. Most importantly, though, he saw the need to be made to feel safe and secure. That was something that he felt everyone deserved, but he also felt that if a male was expected to provide that, then the female should be able to offer the reassurance and support that Shanira was unable to provide.

"That wouldn't be proper. And I didn't come prepared to stay out in Serah tonight," Kai said, trying to speak logic into the current, awkward situation. Staying in the Fire Kingdom wasn't appealing to him at all. And he knew that there would be rumors that would spread like wildfire, literally, if he did stay. Shanira laying on his shoulder was bad enough, he refused to make matters any worse, for her, or himself.

"Well, just come in for a little while? You can hold me until I fall asleep and ease out."

"Good night, Shanira," Kai offered, leaning down. Shanira closed her eyes, awaiting a kiss on the lips. When she felt his eyes land on her cheek, her eyes snapped open.

Without another word, she turned her back to him and snatched the door open. Stomping into the room heavily, she left imprints of her retreating footsteps scorched into the ground. Kai rubbed his hands through his hair, loosening the braids, shaking them free until they fell against his shoulders. Walking back to the carriage, he couldn't be more eager to get home. He was happy that both their kingdoms were within close proximity of each other.

When the carriage pulled up to the Water Kingdom, Kai moved out of the carriage with such haste that he splashed all over the driver, who did nothing but laugh. He's heard at least some of what Shanira was saying and could completely understand Kai's joy to be done with her.

Heading to his bedroom, Kai decided that he'd meet with Kari later. He didn't want to think of his date with Miss Hot and Heavy, as his mother called her. For all the torture and trouble that he endured, he could have at least gotten lucky, the thought came to him, but he dismissed it immediately after. *Nah,* he thought to himself, *as annoying as she is, she still doesn't deserve to be treated like a sex toy.*

Chapter Four

One Down

When Kai returned to his room, his head swimming with frustration, Kari was waiting on him. He wasted no time losing his form. He wanted to get out of anything that reminded him of his date that night. Shanira frustrated him to no end. He couldn't imagine life with her as a mate. He said very little but could see Kari smirking at him from across the room.

"She wants you, you know," Kai shared the obvious with his friend.

"She can give up on that, she's not my type," Kari scoffed at the thought.

"Oh, I know," Kai couldn't help but share a laugh with his friend, "she doesn't have fins and gills or rhythm," he quipped, pointing out one of her more obvious flaws, her inability to dance.

"Yeah, fluidity of movement is not her strong suit," Kari agreed.

"Neither is humility or compromise," Kai pointed out, reminiscing over their date.

Both boys laughed. Shanira truly was a piece of work. They both went over their notes from the evening, Kai deciding, to Kari's agreement, that she was definitely not in the running for the seat on the throne that she was so certain was already hers.

"I can't wait to see her face at the Announcement Ceremony," Kari puffed laughter.

"She needs a lesson in modesty," Kai concluded, and, though that wasn't the main reason for him not choosing her, it would be a wonderful perk.

The boys fell silent, each in their own thoughts. They knew that, even though Shanira would benefit from a lesson in humility, it could be more of a problem than a joy. Kai was grateful for the silence, because it allowed him to wind down from the night from hell. The sound of water flowing down the corridor caught his attention, and he was hoping that it wasn't someone coming to summon him on his father's behalf. He wasn't trying to face Suavai right now and be questioned about the date. He knew that, even though his father wanted him to be happy, the well-being of the kingdom and the realm was more important to him. And rightfully so.

Keeping his eyes on the door, Kai was relieved when Ava flowed gracefully into the room. She had kelp and the latest recording of the Whale Orchestra in hand. Kai stopped talking to Kari and took a moment to admire his mother. She was so regal. Some things can't be taught. Poise and grace were two of them, and Shanira probably wouldn't have taken them seriously, seeing no use for them in the grand scheme of things.

"Oh, Kari," Ava said, surprised to see her son's dear friend, "I didn't know you were here."

"I'm just leaving, Your Highness," Kari darted over to give her a swift kiss on the cheek.

"Are you sure? There's plenty of kelp for everyone and the Whale Orchestra..."

"I'm sure," Kari interrupted her. "I ate enough at the ball tonight and I'm not really a fan of the Whale Orchestra," he admitted.

"Not a fan?" Ava responded, jokingly, as if her feelings were hurt. "You have no idea what you're missing."

"I think I'll keep missing out on that!" Kari quipped in response. They all laughed as Kari took his leave.

"Round Two tomorrow," Kari said to Kai, spinning on his own bursts of laughter out the door.

Kai didn't even attempt to respond. His friend was enjoying his plight a bit too much. But, he knew he would tease Kari the same way if their roles were reversed. Ava smiled at her son as his friend exited the room.

"I'm glad you have your friend to help you make this decision so that you don't have to go through this alone," she smiled her relief. Kai wanted to be surprised that his mother knew what they were doing, but he knew that his mother knew *everything*. She made it her business. Not in the nosy, gossipy kind of way, though. She just felt that it was important to always know what was going in so that she could properly prepare and protect her family and loved ones. And by loved ones that meant everyone in the elemental realm *and* on Earth.

"So am I," Kai agreed, taking some kelp. He chewed it slowly, thoughtfully.

"Miss Hot and Heavy has your molecules off-kilter, huh?" Ava asked. She had known that her son would be flustered after the date with Shanira.

"She's certain that she will be chosen," Kai explained to his mother, "she has the plan all made of how the marriage will go, where we will live, and that we will only have one child," he shifted back and forth in his explanation, clasping as waves into himself. Just the thought of the way Shanira had handled him was beginning a tsunami within him. He was royalty, just as she, but she was acting like she was doing him a favor by entertaining him at all.

"Her father is pretty certain of it, as well," Ava revealed his premature and overly confident statements about his Shanira, the soon-to-be Realm Queen, during the Discussions.

"The look on their faces will be priceless," she continued, giggling a bit at the thought.

"Indeed it will," Kai stated, his inner turmoil obvious to his mother.

"The Treaty states that you have to marry one of the Princesses, and that she will be of *your* choosing," Ava reminded Kai. "That clause was my doing, so that you would not feel totally powerless in your obligation."

"Why couldn't Kari have been the first-born son?" Kai asked, wishing this was his friend's lot and not his. Not that he wished it on his best friend, or anyone. Marrying out of obligation was an age-old tradition. One that his parents had pioneered the change of in their union. Now their son was being forced into that archaic way of life, and it wasn't fair, even if it was for the greater good.

"Because we would definitely all be doomed, and another war would break out when he shunned the rest of the Realm and married a mermaid, or even a dolphin," his mother joked.

Kai vibrated with laughter.

"The responsibility was placed in the right place," Ava assured her son. Even knowing that he was vexed, she hoped that he would see just how powerful he was. She may have been a bit biased, but Ava thought her son to be the handsomest, most level-headed of the five, second only to Makani, whom she hoped he would choose. She would definitely choose her for him, if it were up to her.

"I suppose," Kai stated, still reluctant about it all, "I've got two dates to go. Hopefully, I can find someone like you," he smiled at his mother, reaching for more kelp.

"You will," Ava reassured her son. She knew something that he didn't know. She knew that his love was going to be found in the most unexpected place. But, she also knew, that her son needed to go through this journey and make this choice for himself. It wasn't up to her, or anyone else. And in that, he would find his power.

Ava and Kai settled in, eating kelp and listening to the Whale Orchestra. He would be courting Lurra tomorrow. He needed all the peace he could get tonight.

*****

"I got this shit in the bag," Shanira bragged to Lurra. She was sitting at the vanity in her room, admiring herself in the mirror. She was preparing for the festivities that were being held in honor of her successful courtship with Kai. She'd fabricated the truth quite a bit when she returned home. She didn't want to admit that things didn't go as planned and have her father Afi handle things for her. It was time she started handling things for herself.

Lurra watched her, admiring how beautiful she was. She hated hearing about their courtship but knew that it was out of her hands. And it wasn't like Shanira would give her a second glance anyway. She had chanced coming out into the heat of

Serah when Shanira called her, because she was always there for her friend. She had no plans to stay for the party. Not that her kind was welcome there anyway.

"So it went well, huh?" Lurra asked softly, hiding her sadness.

"Well, yes and no," Shanira admitted. There was no one else that she trusted like she did Lurra. She could be open and honest with her. Lurra was her best friend. Yeah, she knew she had a little crush on her. But she didn't let that take away from the friendship.

"What do you mean, yes and no?" Lurra asked, perking up. She hated that she was excited about her friend not becoming the Queen of the Realm, but she didn't think she could see her being someone else's mate, even if they would never be together.

"Don't sound so excited," Shanira turned to face Lurra with an eye roll. "And I mean, I thought I could talk some sense into him and we were just going to lay out the way things would go. I mean, it's understood that we are going to be rulers of the realm, so I didn't understand why he wasn't onboard."

"So, by talking sense into him, you pretty much tried to boss him around and it didn't work," Lurra said with a chuckle. She knew her friend well, and Shanira only had two levels, hot and scorching. She was an acquired taste, and very few could tolerate her. In reality, she was just misunderstood, but she didn't let people get close enough to see the her that wasn't the spoiled Fire Princess.

"Don't do me, L," Shanira said, becoming annoyed. She was about to regret inviting her into her space, but she needed someone there. She hated being alone, especially when she felt uncomfortable. And Kai's rejection made her feel helpless and unattractive. What better way to bolster her self-esteem than have Lurra come and stare at her with that glazed over look in her eyes?

"See, the real issue is that Kai didn't *do you*," Lurra spoke truth. She was in her feelings and her words betrayed her.

"Tell me how you really feel, Lurra. You're just upset because *you* can't do me," Shanira clapped back.

"And that's my cue," Lurra sighed, dropping her head. She hated the way Shanira handled her sometimes. She treated her like she wasn't the only friend she had in the entire realm. Her feelings were hurt, and with all that was going on with the Courtships and her dreaded date with Kai coming soon, she wasn't looking to be attacked by Shanira just because her pride was bruised.

"I'm sorry, L. Please don't leave me," Shanira begged, becoming transparent again.

"You're not sorry, Shanira. You never are. You just don't want to be left alone. But here's a piece of advice," Lurra snapped, her hand on the door to the room. She turned around to look at Shanira to make sure that her words were heard. "That vanity you're sitting at, turn and face that mirror and consider that *vanity* may just be your problem."

Turning and pulling the door open with all her might, she left Shanira's room, only able to hold the sap that was trying to streak down her cheeks until she had walked away.

"Fine! I don't need you, Lurra! If you were half the powerful being I was, you'd be vain, too. There's nothing wrong with having confidence," Shanira stood in her doorway yelling at Lurra's back.

"See, that's the thing. Confidence is silent. Insecurities are loud," Lurra said, turning around angrily facing Shanira, not caring if she saw the sap leaking from her eyes. "You're *not* confident, and everyone in the realm knows it but you. Get to know yourself, Shanira, and you'll see why no one else has any desire to get to know you."

"You do," Shanira hollered, not wanting to lose the argument.

"Correction, I *did*," Lurra checked Shanira. She walked away, heading to her room slowly. She and Shanira argued often, but never as badly as this. She didn't think they could come back from this. Especially since Shanira had shown no concern for Lurra's pain that was pouring down her face.

The trek home was a long one. The sap that Lurra couldn't stop from leaking from her eyes and onto the ground bloomed into kudzu, evident that her pain was consuming her like the plant consumed anything in the path of its growth.

Finally getting home, she climbed into the window she'd snuck out of, knowing that her parents would be terribly upset if they found out that she'd risked her well-being to be there for Shanira. Once she was settled in, Lurra ran some cold water to clean the sticky substance from her face before stepping into the waterfall that had been setup in her lavatory to wash the wax off of her body that protected her from the Orange Star's heat. Once cleaned, she laid down. She tried to mentally prepare herself for her Courtship with Kai and accept what may have been the end of her friendship with Shanira.

Shanira stomped back into her room, shooting a fireball into the door to close it. The wood being prepared for Serah was the only reason that it didn't burst into flame. She didn't take Lurra's advice and face her reflection. Instead, she laid down, deciding that her friend was just in her feelings about everything that was going on and being emotional. Just like Lurra knew Shanira, she knew Lurra as well. And she knew that, underneath that hollow exterior, she was as delicate as a rose petal. Tensions and emotions were high with everyone right now. The Courtships could make or break everything as they all knew it. So, she would let her friend calm down, and then they would be back like they'd never left. She was sure of it. That was just how things went with them.

Getting dressed, she went out to celebrate with the rest of her Kingdom. She planned to eat, drink, and get into some mischief. There was no better validation than that of those you reigned over. And depending how drunk she got, she might just take some unsuspecting being to help ease her loneliness, and reinvigorate her confidence and certainty that she was, in fact, appealing and attractive.

Temperatures Rising

Kai was beginning to be able to tell the difference between Danksha and Serah. His temperature was higher than usual, something he knew would have been far worse had they not taken every precaution to shield the Kingdom from the Orange Sun's Light. Before he could completely awaken, Kari blew in, probably fresh out of a Merlesque Lounge. Kai wondered where he got the energy sometimes. Kari swirled around him, filling the air with mist.

He was cooling himself off. Although he knew of the dangers of being in the Orange Star's heat for too long, he refused to be restrained. His father had pointed out, some time ago, that they were the only element, other than Fire, that could sustain and not be permanently destroyed during Serah. This was the one truth that the Fire Kingdom didn't want anyone else to discover. So they painted the Wind Kingdom as weak and unreliable, uncertain. They were not taken seriously. But, Kari knew that the meaning of the saying, "every which way the wind blows" had a different connotation than the one that was used to discredit his Kingdom. Instead of showing lack of stability, it was truly a sign of the power of the wind. They could control anything. Make it go where it wanted to, do what it wanted to.

"Do I even want to *know* what you're thinking right now?" Kai asked his friend, stirring him from a stillness that he'd rarely experienced from his friend. And, do I want to know what you got yourself into last night?"

Kai knew that, whether he wanted to know or not, Kari was going to share every sordid detail about his night. What he hadn't expected, however, was *who* he would admit to being with.

"Probably not," Kari responded.

His response took Kai aback because it was so out of character for his friend. This was usually when Kari would spill the beans about the mermaid he'd spent the night with, filling her gills with himself. How her scales felt. But not today. Today, Kari moved through the room slowly, somberly, as if cooling his temperature had brought him to his senses. Kai thought he saw a hint of shame or remorse in his friend's face. His currents were certainly off.

"Everything alright?" Kai asked, suddenly concerned about his friend.

"Yeah," Kari responded.

"Wanna talk about it?" Kai offered, for the first time actually interested in Kari's antics from the previous night. He wanted to know what could possibly make his conscienceless friend act in such a way.

"I don't... know," Kari responded, knowing that he should, but feeling badly for betraying his friend.

"You're always here for me, Kari," Kai urged, "tell me what's going on."

"Ok," Kari finally conceded, "but hear me out, ok?" He asked his friend.

"Sure," Kai responded, settling in to listen to the tale.

"There was a party in the Fire Kingdom last night," Kari explained, "they were awaiting Shanira's return and celebrating what they called 'their time to shine,' because of their being able to prosper during Serah while the rest of us can't," he said, pausing to look at his friend's face.

"Well, it's not like they are known for their tact or humility," Kai said, shaking his head and thinking of the conversation he and Kari had just had the previous night.

"Shanira came back with reports of a good date and great negotiations made between the two of you," Kari went on, not wanting to lose his nerve, "she didn't know I was there watching the two of you, so I didn't say anything because I didn't want to ruin our plan."

"Understandable," Kai confirmed, knowing there was more.

"I was out of my element, but they really know how to party, and you know how I love a good party," Kari continued, beating around the bush.

Kai said nothing, but he had a feeling he knew what was about to come next.

"Have you ever had ambrosia warm," Kari asked, rhetorically, "it makes it so much more potent. One minute, I was dancing with this light chick, when Shanira cut in. It was different from the ball. I had one shot too many of scorched ambrosia, as they called it, and allowed her to breathe me."

Kai wasn't as shocked as Kari expected. There were slight ripples in his surface, but Kari had expected a wave. He wanted his friend to be upset about his betrayal. Kai's calmness was unnerving. It caused Kari to begin to lose form, becoming clouds of self. He decided to continue with his confession.

"I truly apologize for this, Kai," Kari stated, "I feel guilty, because I know that you just courted her and, although she isn't in the running for you after your Courtship last night, dependent on how the next two Courtships go, she may be your wife. For the sake of alliance and the Treaty. But," he continued, "What's worse is, I liked it," Kari admitted.

Kai laughed, thwacking into himself. His friend had fallen into Shanira's trap. But she had been after him. And Shanira usually got what Shanira wanted.

"So, you like her?" he asked his lifelong friend, who had become nothing but stillness within the room.

"I don't know," Kari's confusion was apparent, "she's so selfish. She's short-sighted and full of herself. She's full of her own power. But," he admitted, "I can't deny that what happened last night was spectacular. It was like nothing I have ever felt before, even with all of my trysts with the maids and dolphins, the limbs and nymphs. This," he paused, embarrassed, "was different."

"Well, you two do benefit one another," Kai rationalized, "and all of the flaws that you mentioned sound like someone else I know," he said with a laugh.

"Who?" Kari asked, completely shocked, yet appreciative of his friend's response to the situation.

Kai laughed even harder, thunder rolling through the room with every jovial clap, "YOU," he said between laughs. "Sounds to me like you've met your match," Kai concluded.

"But what about your Courtship?" Kari asked.

"You said it yourself, I have no interest in pursuing any kind of union with Shanira, arranged or otherwise," he said emphatically. "But, again," he explained, "it sounds like *you* may have found your match."

Kai burst into laughter again, as Kari regained form, relieved that he had not caused a problem in their friendship. More importantly, he was happy that his actions had not led to another war. He'd heard that the last Serah war had been about a girl.

Chapter Six

On Solid Ground

Once the confession was out in the open, Kari was able to focus on helping Kai prepare for his Courtship of Lurra. They laughed at the fact that they thought she was more interested in her own gender than theirs. She was Shanira's flunky. Followed her around and answered to her every beck and call. They were certain there was more to her devotion than mere friendship. But it was something that remained unspoken.

Kai's court setup the dates, so he had no idea what to expect. He hoped that it would be something that they both would enjoy, that wouldn't call for much interaction. He'd had his fill of that with Shanira the night before. He hoped that she was the worst of his choices, she was definitely the most flamboyant, but you never knew what a date and the potential of ruling the realm may bring out of anyone.

Kai didn't get very dressed up. He knew that, whatever he and Lurra got into, it would be laid back and fun. He liked her well enough, just wasn't interested in her romantically. They had lots of fun planning and carrying out the weather cycles. She was so knowledgeable of Earth and kept detailed notes of what areas needed water and which ones did not. The rain forests and desert oases were their doing. They used to play together quite frequently when they were children. But, in his eyes, she was more like Kari than someone he could spend his life with.

When it was time to leave, Kai told Kari to sit this one out.

"There are no notes to take on this one, Kari," he explained, "you know this one isn't going anywhere," he laughed as he shifted into his simplest form, his hair not even spiked. He pulled it into a ponytail instead and donned a simple rippled demeanor.

"You sure?" Kari asked, a bit offended and afraid that his friend may actually be a bit upset with him about the Shanira incident.

"Yeah," he confirmed, "and you need to get some rest. You've been up all night."

There was no maliciousness in his tone. He was genuinely concerned about his friend. They left together, planning to meet the next day so that Kai could fill Kari in on the events of the evening and prepare for his Courtship of Makani.

"Maybe you can sneak Makani's diary and give me some pointers," Kai joked. He had no idea that his friend took his request very seriously. They embraced one another in a brotherly hug that shook the ripples in Kai's demeanor and made Kai's hair lay down from the humidity.

"Aight, man. Go rest," he ordered Kari again, pushing him away. "Done wrinkled my 'fit and everything. Just because I don't want Lurra doesn't mean that I don't wanna be my most debonair when I pick her up."

Laughing, there was a bit of relief in Kari's demeanor. He was worried about his friend being upset with him. He'd never known Kai to be passive aggressive, but this was a different, extremely touchy situation. He could tell now that Kai meant it when he said he was good. He wasn't going to promise that he wasn't going to watch Kai's courtship with Lurra, but once it was over, at least he would be able to rest easily, knowing that he hadn't lost his dearest friend with his reckless actions.

Kai was surprised that he was met outside with a Pegasus instead of a carriage for this date. He was starting to realize more and more that his mother was the one at the helm of planning all the Courtships. The sushi and Squid Ink Wine and Humpback Whale riding should've been a dead giveaway, but riding a Pegasus, something that he'd loved to do since he was a child, had definitely confirmed it for him.

Kneeling in reverence to Kai, the Pegasus allowed him to pet its nose so that Kai knew it wasn't threatened by him. Stroking its mane, the Pegasus lowered its head, allowing Kai to climb up onto its back. As if knowing where it was headed, the Pegasus whisked into the air, Kai's ponytail flapping around his face in the wind. He loved the feel of the air against his surface. It was an awesome feeling. Landing on a cloud, the Pegasus lowered its head, kneeling down as it had done before so that Kai could get down. Petting the Pegasus to show his appreciation, he smiled when it bowed to him once again and dove off the cloud.

Seeing the picnic laid out for them, Kai could only imagine what the basket held for them. Not letting his curiosity get the best of him, he decided to wait for Lurra, so that they could open the basket together. Laying on the cloud with his hands laced behind his head, the calm stillness was relaxing. Kai was almost asleep when he felt a gust and knew that Kari was being hard-headed and was somewhere nearby. Closing his eyes back with a chuckle, he waited for Lurra's arrival.

Lurra held the Pegasus that had been sent to pick her up to meet Kai for their Courtship on a bed of clouds in the corner of the Realm. She became nervous when she saw the picnic that had been laid out for them. Hearing the neigh of the Pegasus made Kai stand to his feet. Seeing a terrified Lurra gripping the Pegasus so tightly he was wondering how the poor thing could breathe, he stepped back to give them a clear space for landing. When the Pegasus came to a stop, lowering so that Lurra could get down, Kai helped her down, smiling that she was shaking.

Giving her a few moments to compose herself, he petted the Pegasus, giving it permission to leave. Looking at Lurra, Kai was taken aback by her outfit. She was covered in oak leaves in the shape of a mini-dress. She wore a fully bloomed lotus behind her ear. Kai couldn't help but notice the thickness of her thighs. He couldn't remember ever seeing them exposed before.

"You ok?" Lurra asked Kai, noticing his uncharacteristic silence.

"Yes, it's just, you look beautiful," he complimented, making her blue a powder pink under her wooded flesh.

"Thank you," Lurra blushed harder.

"You're welcome. But since I'm stating the obvious, I should be asking you if you're ok. You almost strangled that poor Pegasus. I'm sure he didn't expect to almost die when he agreed to this task," he teased, lightening the mood, and diverting his eyes from her body.

"You're not funny, KaiThar," she called him by his full name. "Who thought of this mess? I'm terribly afraid of heights," she admitted.

"But the trees," Kai pointed out, unsure how she could be afraid of heights with all the varying elevation her people encountered on a regular basis.

"That's different. There's always some ground somewhere. I'm not ok when my feet can't touch the ground. And we're far from the ground up here."

"Understood," Kai nodded, understanding where she was coming from. "But you're safe up here," he promised.

"Why? Because I'm with you?" she asked, mushing his head playfully.

"But of course," he joked back, hooking his arm that she took hesitantly so that she could lead them to the picnic.

They sat and ate, laughing and talking about their plans for the upcoming Spring. It was Lurra's favorite Season. She lit up talking about the way that the creatures brought forth life and the vegetation grew. How she loved to see vegetation growing on and through stone and that it was a mark of strength to be able to bloom is an environment that was outside of their norm.

"That means that they dig their roots deep enough into the stone to *find* soil and water," she explained excitedly, "that nothing can tell them where they didn't belong and what they weren't capable of."

Kai just listened. He liked Lurra's excitement about the Land, the Earth. She was going to be the perfect ruler of her Kingdom because she shared a true connection with all of the beasts and creatures, she showed no favoritism, and took pride in her ability to take such good care of them.

"You're going to be a *great* Land Queen, Lurra," Kai encouraged, "you truly do have a passion for the Earth."

Lurra blushed. "Thank you, Kai," she said, caught off-guard by the compliment, her blush returning.

Kai, himself was surprised at how beautiful Lurra truly was when she softened her expressions.

"I'm hoping that we can maintain our alliance once you and Shanira are married," she said, in a softened tone.

Kai could hear the concern in her voice, telling him that she really didn't feel like she could rely on her friend to look out for her. Kai reached out and touched her hand, his moisture seeping into the pores of her wood.

"Regardless of the outcome of these Courtships," Kai advised her earnestly, "the alliance with the Land Kingdom will remain intact. As a matter of fact, I would like to hear your ideas on how we can better unite all four of the Kingdoms."

Lurra giggled. No one ever asked her about her ideas. She had books and books of them in her room.

"Welllllll, since you asked..." she responded before diving into her extensive plans, showing Kai a side of her that he'd never seen before. She was wise and insightful. She had a clairvoyance and understanding that came from being connected to all that was around her, not just in her kingdom, but on Earth as well.

Listening to her, he couldn't help but wonder how she was friends with Shanira. They were polar opposites. But then he realized that so were he and Kari, and they were as thick as thieves. They spent the rest of their evening, and the rest of the date, discussing ways to make things better for everyone.

Chapter Seven

Love Hurts

Lurra had opted to be dropped off at the edge of her Kingdom so that she could walk the remainder of the way home. She had a lot on her mind. The conversations with Kai made her feel like she was more relevant than she'd felt her entire life. The way he embraced her ideas and let her lead the conversation was new for her. She wanted to attribute it to him being charismatic, but there was nothing romantic about their date. Aside from the compliments, that she knew were genuine because she knew Kai didn't waste words, he had respected her for her mind and knowledge. She could tell that he was going to make someone a great partner. Even though she hoped, and he told her without saying, that it wouldn't be her. She was relieved by that, honestly, and skipped her way through the forest on her way home.

"So," Shanira asked Lurra. Catching up to her on the way home after their date. Blowing out a frustrated breath, she wasn't in the mood for Shanira. She hadn't fully forgiven her for their last fight, and still wasn't sure if she wanted to be bothered with Shanira anymore at all.

"So what?" Lurra quipped back, not wanting to share all of the details of their date with her friend.

"Did he say that he had chosen me?" Shanira asked, her narcissism showing little concern for the actual events of her friend's date. Seeing this frustrated Lurra even more. She had just been on her Courtship, and Shanira was dismissively approaching her like she knew there was no chance of Kai choosing Lurra. She wasn't even able to offer an ear about how the date had gone, good or bad, like Lurra had just done for her the night before.

"I didn't ask," Lurra replied, honestly, trying to move around Shanira. She was over the conversation already.

"Well, what have the two of you been up to all this time?" Shanira asked, disinterestedly.

She couldn't wrap her mind around the thought that they had talked about anything but her. That was what she'd asked Lurra to do before the Courtships began; to help her sell herself as the only true option as being Kai's mate. Lurra had agreed, so she didn't understand why things had changed. More than anything, she *knew* how close Lurra and Kai were, so next to Kari, she was the best person to persuade Kai that Shanira was the best choice.

When she didn't get the response she wanted, or any response at all, she blocked Lurra, preventing her from going any further. She shined light on her bark and realized that she was glistening.

"Did you... merge with my future king, you tramp?" Shanira demanded.

"You mean, like you merged with his best friend last night?" Lurra pointed out, shocking Shanira that she knew of her actions at the Fire Party the night before. "No, I didn't."

Not feeling like Shanira deserved an answer, she gave her one anyway. There was no need to lie about what had happened between her and Kai. What they'd done was better than any merging could have been. Kai had shown Lurra that he valued her as a Princess and future ruler with innovative thoughts. Thoughts that Shanira had never cared enough to listen to. Kai had been a real friend to Lurra, and that was something that she'd never had.

"That was different, Lurra," Shanira struggled to explain, "it was nothing. Really."

"Nothing? I *love* you. I have been devoted to you and watch you as you merge with dignitaries from all across the Realm. I have even accepted that you and Kai will marry because it is the best thing for the Realm, that you will bear him an heir. But *Kari*, there was no reason for that to transpire last night. I always saw the way you looked at him. I know that *he* is truly the best suited match for you, but I never thought that you would... *betray me*, the way that you did." Lurra's hurt was apparent in her speech.

"Oh, I get it," Shanira smirked, "so, you merged with my future husband as revenge?"

"You truly don't get it at all," Lurra sighed, realizing that her affections had been one-sided all this time.

She started to walk away but Shanira grabbed her arm, scorching her bark.

"Don't you walk away from me," she flared.

"Let me go, Shanira!" Lurra yelped in pain. "You're hurting me!"

"That was my intention, Lurra. Geez, are you that basic?" Shanira insulted. "I'll let you go when I see fit. You need to realize that you belong to me and," she leaned in closely to Lurra, so close that her bark began to splint, "you will *not* leave me, or ruin my becoming Queen of this Realm, or you and your beloved Kingdom may not survive it."

Looking back and forth from the blaze burning in Shanira's eyes and the burning bark that was her wrist, she was becoming more and more afraid by the moment. The viciousness in Shanira's expression frightened Lurra. She knew that she wasn't kidding.

"If you betray me, your demise will be slow... and painful."

Shanira released her arm, which had been scorched so badly that it would take weeks of treatment with mud and leaves to heal it. Lurra watched her walk away in a fury, singeing everything she touched on the way back to her Kingdom.

Lurra stopped and wrapped her arm. She could barely see to patch herself up because of the sap leaking from her eyes. She knew that Shanira was hotheaded, but she would've never thought that she would cause her any real harm. This was a side of Shanira that even she hadn't seen. She was drunk with her own power and determined to obtain the throne by any means. Once patched up, she made herself a shawl from moss hanging from a tree she passed on the way home. The last thing she wanted to do was alarm her parents, and she definitely didn't want them to think that Kai had been the one to hurt her.

"How did it go?" Fanua, her mother asked, she had been waiting up for her daughter's return. They talked about everything. She knew that her child preferred the fairer gender, and although it would be great to have her as the Queen of the Realm, she knew that Lurra would make a great ruler, whether it be of their Kingdom, or the entire realm.

"It was fine," Lurra said, hating that her mother had waited up on her.

She knew she would and any other time, they would sip rose hip sundaes and she would be dishing about the great time she'd had with her friend Kai. Instead, she wanted to get to her room as quickly as possible without her mother seeing her injury.

"Just fine? Lurra? LURRA!" Fanua yelled behind her daughter, swiftly getting up from her seat on her favorite stump.

Lurra kept moving, knowing that getting to her room was the only way to get some privacy until she could come up with an explanation that wouldn't cause chaos in the realm. She was almost there when she ran into the chest of her father, Luga, who had come out of his room to find out why his wife was yelling. Alarmed when he realized that she was calling their child, he quickened his pace, meeting Lurra in the corridor a few steps from her room.

"Lurra, what's wrong?" he asked, concerned.

"Nothing," she lied. "I just want to lay down."

"No, tell us what happened," Luga's voice boomed, startling his wife and daughter. He was a mild-mannered being, so raising his voice was out of character.

Hanging her head, Lurra knew that she was going to have to tell them something. Even though Shanira had hurt her, she didn't want to get her in trouble. Nor did she want her father or mother going to the Fire Kingdom and getting hurt. Reaching her daughter and husband, Fanua stood beside Luga, studying Lurra. Taking inventory of her daughter's appearance, she seemed unharmed. After a moment, Fanua noticed that there was something different in her dress from the outfit she'd left in. Pulling back the moss, she gasped, and her eyes immediately began to leak at the sight of her daughter's arm.

"Did Kai—" Fanua started, but Luga cut her off.

"I'll destroy him!" Luga yelled, pushing past his daughter, headed out of their kingdom.

"Papa, no! It wasn't Kai!" Lurra yelled, grabbing her father's arm with her injured one. She grimaced and let go, but she'd stopped Luga in his steps.

"Then who?" Fanua started and Lurra fell silent, rubbing her hurting arm.

Her daughter's silence was all the confirmation she needed, and Luga knew as well. He knew there was one person that she would protect with her life, and she hated that she cared for such a selfish being the way she did.

"Fanua, tend to our child. I have a matter to handle."

Without another word, or waiting for a response, Luga left them in the corridor and they soon heard the door slam closed with so much force that it made them both jump. Both women wept, Fanua taking Lurra to the lavatory to clean up and re-patch her wound. Neither of them spoke, both in their own thoughts. Fanua was sending love and calm to her husband. Luga was a gentle giant of a man and she had only seen him upset once before. That time had caused the onset of the First Realm War. She needed him to be more level-headed this time around, but she knew that he was going to protect his family to his death.

Lurra was thinking of what needed to be done to head off another Realm War. She planned to tell Kai what had happened the next day, because she knew that Shanira not getting her way could definitely mean danger for the entire Realm. She just hoped that her father didn't act rashly before she could get to Kai.

When her mother finished with her wound, Lurra hugged her tightly before going to her room to change into something more comfortable. She was restless and knew trying to sleep was pointless. Leaving to go to her treehouse, the place she went when she needed to think. When she climbed the rope ladder, she was shocked to see her father there, deep in thought. The relief that he hadn't gone and done something dangerous filled her, but she couldn't stand to see his shoulders hunched in defeat.

"I'll handle it, Papa," she promised him, wrapping her arms around his massive shoulders. He was a handsome creature with a rigid jaw but the kindest eyes. He looked at her with a certainty that she hadn't expected.

"I know. And this is your battle to fight. I believe in you," he said, the pain evident in his voice. "I've raised you to be a Queen, a ruler. Use your mind and you'll defeat those who react without thinking," he said, standing but having to bend down because he was too tall to stand up in the treehouse. He kissed his daughter on the cheek before leaving to return to the house, sure that his wife was sick with worry.

"Thank you, Papa," Lurra was grateful to have his vote of confidence. It was time for her generation to handle things, and after her Courtship with Kai, and now her father's words, she knew that she was ready to do what was necessary. Sitting alone in the treehouse, she meditated on several things. The most important being letting go of any affection she had for Shanira— friendship or otherwise.

Chapter Eight

Gone with The Wind

Kai woke up with flurries. He couldn't hide his excitement about the Courtship with Makani. He kept thinking back to the ball and how their dance had been so seamless, so effortless. How beautiful she'd looked. It felt strange to feel this way about his best friend's twin sister. He put that thought out of his mind and started preparing for his Courtship. He couldn't decide whether to wear Koi like he had the night of the ball or something less formal, like a clown fish or jellyfish. A shark or a sting ray would show his power. He remembered, when he was young, his father teaching him how to maintain form with life inside of him. He remembered how it tickled. How his father had told him it would come in handy one day. Now, Kai prided himself in the ability to maintain form while several creatures swam through him.

Kai was plagued with decisions. He even wanted to do something different with his hair. As he paced, trying to settle on something, he was surprised when his mother came through the door. She must have been standing there watching him for some time, because she couldn't control the waves of laughter when she finally entered the room.

"So, Makani is the one, huh?" She asked her son, seeing his shift in behavior.

"I think so, I mean, I don't know," he replied nervously, "there was something there between us at the ball but, I haven't spoken to Makani in ages. I don't know anything about her."

"You should ask her brother," she suggested, "I'm sure Kari would love to do some reconnaissance on her. It would give him a reason to go through her things, and that's what little brothers *live* for." She laughed again at the thought. "Your Uncle Renthro did it to me for your father. Lucky for him, I already liked him."

"Dad needed help," Kai asked, shocked, "I can't even imagine him being insecure," he admitted.

"Insecure is a kind way of putting it. He was goofy. Uncomfortable in himself. He didn't want the Kingdom or the responsibility that came with it. You get that from him, by the way," she chuckled, currents flowing through her.

Kai smirked at the thought of it all. But he couldn't understand, then, why his father would put the pressure of the Treaty on him if he knew what it felt like to hate responsibility.

"He was the one that pushed the Courtship Clause, Kai," his mother advised him, knowing what her son was thinking, "the Treaty was necessary, but we still wanted you to have some say in the matter. Without him, Afi would've dismissed my suggestion."

Kai couldn't help realizing that the Fire Kingdom had been a big problem for the realm for a very long time. He made a mental note to speak with Kari and Lurra about ways to end that tradition. In this moment, though, he breathed a sigh of relief. He was grateful that his mother shared this with him. It made things easier to know that his father, a man he respected so greatly, had also felt the apprehension that he was feeling right now.

"So," Ava asked, "what are you thinking of wearing tonight for your *big date*," she teased.

"Mom, I have no idea. I'm nervous. I want to make a great first impression, but I don't want it to go to waste it if she's not into me like that. I mean, she's the Wind Princess. She may not want all of this responsibility, you know," Kai opened up to his mother.

"Regardless of her Kingdom, son, she's a Princess and will govern over someone. She's older than Kari, yes?" she asked.

"Yes," Kai confirmed.

"For all you know, she may be *ready* for this kind of responsibility. As far as impressions, don't put on a façade for her. Just be yourself. If she likes you, she'll like *you*, not someone you're pretending to be..."

"And she *does* like you," Kari gusted in, interjecting himself into the conversation, "a lot."

"Kari," Ava greeted him with a smile and a quick hug.

"Your Highness," Kari nodded, pulling away, before shooting his friend his widest grin.

"She's been up all night planning for this Courtship," Kari revealed. "Her diary exposed that she has been waiting on it for a minute now. You wanna see?" he offered, holding the diary that he'd stolen from his sister out in Kai's face.

"I don't condone this, but I have to say that it's a bit déjà vu-ish," Ava stated, shaking her head, remembering Renthro stealing her diary and giving it to Suavai to read. Or, as they'd called it, "do a little research".

Kari was taking obvious pleasure in knowing that his sister had been crushing on his best friend all this time. He was also excited about the fact that Kai liked her as well and, if they ended up together, he knew she would be well cared for and loved. It was a weight off of his shoulders as her brother.

Kai gave him a baffled expression. The ripples in his form were becoming rifts and waves as he realized that he may have found his Queen.

"She likes your hair down, says she likes the *flow* of it. Says it's adorable when it falls into your face," Kari shared, barely able to contain himself, "and her favorite fish is jellyfish, so you may want to wear some tonight."

Ava called for the servants and had them bring a jellyfish for her son. She also laughed at the fact that all little brothers truly did enjoy invading their sisters' privacy. As they prepared for the evening, Lurra came to the door. She was covered in moist leaves to protect herself from the heat of the Orange Star, and her arm was wrapped and covered with leaves and mud. Apparently, she had been injured.

"Lurra," Kai greeted her, surprised to see her. At the end of their Courtship, they had agreed that she and Kari would be on his Council, so he hoped that she wasn't there to confess some newfound love for him.

"I know you're preparing for your Courtship with Makani, and I apologize for interrupting," Lurra began, "but I have to warn you that Shanira plans to spy on you two tonight," she confessed. "She wants me to come with her and I plan to, just to make sure that she doesn't do anything crazy," she said, looking down at her arm.

"Did she do that to you?" Ava asked, maternally.

"Yes, your Highness," Lurra admitted, embarrassed. "But I'm fine. I just wanted to let Kai know what Shanira was planning and that, if you don't choose her, she may start a war," she spoke hurriedly.

Ava ordered a Doc-Topus to treat Lurra's wounds with algae to accelerate the healing, and the four of them prepared for the worst. Once she was bandaged, and the four of them were alone, Ava proved why she was the Water Queen.

"We have to get ahead of this. I'll call a meeting with the other leaders so that they can be brought up to speed," Ava planned to call a secret meeting with the other Leaders to discuss Shanira's plan. She knew they would have to hold an intervention to make the Afi believe that his perfect little girl was capable of such a thing, but her best friend Pa'u, the Fire Queen, was not fooled by her daughter's charm, so she would be a great help.

"I'll make sure to keep an eye on Shanira," Lurra chimed in, knowing that she could be putting herself in danger.

"Good, and you report back here immediately after the Courtship," Ava said sternly. The mother in her told her that she needed to lay eyes on Lurra to make sure that she wasn't harmed.

"You know I've got your back," Kari promised Kai, patting him on the shoulder. This was the most serious that anyone had seen him, and they had to admit they were impressed. It showed that, if Makani was selected as the Queen of the Realm, he would be able to Rule the Wind Kingdom. He was waiting for Lurra or Kai to doubt his loyalty because of the interactions he'd had with Shanira and the fact that he liked her, but no one did. That let him know that his friends were truly his friends and trusted him with their lives. And he planned to protect them, even if it meant snuffing out the woman that he was catching feelings for.

"I feel like I should be doing more," Kai spoke up, feeling like everyone was doing something important and he wasn't.

"You need to focus on your Courtship," Ava informed him, knowing her son well enough to know that he wasn't going to be ok with being on a date while everyone else prepared for the war. "What you are doing for us all is no easy task. Even though you get to choose, you are still sacrificing yourself for the realm. Let the realm sacrifice for you, too," she reasoned with him, knowing he's at odds.

"Now, go make my sister your queen," Kari gave his friend a reassuring smile. Looking at Ava, Lurra, and Kari, made Kai feel like he was ready to be a ruler. A leader is only as strong as his support system, and he was looking at a support system that was rock solid.

Lurra gave Kai a tight one-armed hug, keeping her damaged arm extended and out of the way and Ava kissed her son's forehead, something that she hadn't done since he was a young child.

"Now, let's get to it," Ava ordered, ushering everyone out of Kai's room.

As they all rushed away to their tasks, Kai was left alone to prepare himself, mentally, for his Courtship. He lost his form, flowing in meditation until he found his serenity. He found peace in the knowledge that he had such great friends in his life and everyone was willing to work together in the best interest of the Kingdom. When he regained his form and followed his escort to the carriage that Makani was in, awaiting him, he felt like the Water King, for the first time. His walk was even different. He was ready.

Makani looked beautiful in a cloudy short set that accentuated her frame. Her hair pulled into a bun on top of her head revealed how much she and Kari actually looked alike.

"A picture would last longer," she snapped, the way he stared at her in the carriage making her uncomfortable. She thought she looked cute, but now, she wasn't so sure.

"Forgive me," he apologized, realizing that he'd been staring at her, and that could be seen as rude. "You just look absolutely beautiful."

"Compared to what? I stay fly," she pointed out, both of them laughing and easing the discomfort of the meaning of their date for the evening.

"True, it's just tonight... I don't know. Tonight, you look like a queen. *My queen*," Kai said, making her currents shift shyly.

"Your queen, huh?" she asked, nothing else sarcastic coming to mind. He had her head gone long before tonight, but he was making it worse by the second. "Well, as your queen, I would like to make my first decree."

"And what's that?" Kai asked, curiously.

"I want to change the plans for our date."

"To what?"

"I wanna go Whale Back riding," she said, making Kai beam from ear-to-ear.

"What my queen wants, my queen gets," he agreed without hesitation. "Driver! Change of plans. My queen," he said, grinning at Makani, loving the way that calling her his queen made her feel. "Would like to go Whale Back riding!"

The carriage rerouted, and soon they were on the beach summoning whales for their ride.

"This is funnnnnn!" Makani yelled over the whoosh of the water as they raced through the ocean. She was looking at Kai, loving the way that his hair kept falling into his face. She thought he was so handsome. He was the mate of her dreams, but she never thought that her dreams would come true.

"What do I get if I beat you back to the beach?" Kai asked Makani with a sly grin.

"What do you want?"

"Your heart," he took the chance to let her know that her love was all that he'd ever wanted. He'd crushed on Makani for what felt like his entire life, but she never gave him any indication that she felt the same way. Now, all the teasing that she'd done throughout their lives made sense.

"Deal!" Makani yelled, patting her Humpback Whale on the head and whispering something in her ear.

The whale took off, leaving Kai far behind, but as soon as they were out of sight, Makani's whale slowed down. Diving into the ocean with Makani on her back, they hid below the water's surface until they felt Kai and his whale pass them. Slowly rising to the surface, as not to be found out, they sped to the beach, getting there a few knots after Kai.

"I thought you'd beat me," Kai said, smiling when he realized that he'd won the race.

"That's what you get for thinking," Makani flirted.

Feeling a vibe, Kai walked up to Makani and kissed her so deeply that they began to create a fog. Releasing her, Kai smiled at her, both of them trying to catch their breath. Grabbing her hand, he pulled her silently back to the carriage. After helping her in, he had a brief conversation with their driver, before joining Makani in the carriage.

"Where to next?" she asked.

"Let's see where the night takes us," Kai said slyly. Makani nodded and leaned back into the seat. She was still floating from their kiss and didn't want the night to end. Kai sat across from her, admiring her. He knew that he would look at her this way for the remainder of their existence.

The sound of music made Makani open her eyes, and she saw Kai staring at her with so much adoration in her eyes. When the carriage stopped, her eyes lit up and she tornado'ed in her seat with excitement until he helped her out of the carriage. The Whale Orchestra rehearsing for the Announcement Ceremony, and they rested in a clearing on the ground, enjoying the music. Kai laid on his back with his fingers beneath his head, and Makani laid in his chest. They enjoyed the music and the closeness; no words being spoken.

The orchestra finished their practice, seemingly too soon for Kai and Makani. They weren't ready for their night to end. They were enjoying themselves so much that Kai hadn't thought about Shanira watching them or the impending doom that the Realm may face.

"Do you see this? He wasn't like that with me," Shanira snapped, looking at Lurra. She caught her smiling and it pissed her off even more. "You're loving this aren't you?"

"No, what are you talking about? I mean, it's sweet, though. You have to admit that they get along well together," Lurra pointed out, hoping to remove any malicious thoughts from Shanira's head.

"It doesn't matter how good they look together. A cute couple doesn't make for the best political pairing," Shanira argued, still feeling that she was the best choice.

Lurra could tell that Shanira felt threatened, and she should've been. It was apparent that Kai had made his choice, and anyone with eyes could tell that they were made for each other. They were born at the same time, which was why Kari was the younger of the twins. The more time that they spent together, the angrier Shanira became, and this alarmed Lurra. But surprisingly, she didn't react, just watched the remainder of their date together.

After the Whale Orchestra, Makani took Kai air skating, where they soared, feet barely touching the water, around the Kingdom. They Cloud hopped, trampolining into the sky, doing tricks and laughing. And, when they had exhausted themselves in all the fun, they settled in or the limb of a tree and talked for hours. They discussed currents and weather shifts, laughed about Kari and his antics. Everything was perfect. Effortless. Without discussing the Announcement in any seriousness at all, they both knew that they were going to rule the Realm together.

Kai wanted to merge with her. And, the way that she looked at him, he could tell the feeling was mutual. The tension in the carriage was thick as it escorted them to the Wind Kingdom when they finally decided to call it a night. Kai knew that he had to touch her, even if they didn't merge. He needed to be close to her. Crossing the carriage and sitting next to Makani, he worked up the nerve to speak.

"May I kiss you," Kai asked permission this time, politely, not wanting to go as far as merging before their marriage but wanting to kiss her again.

"Yes," Makani replied in a wispy tone. She moved the hair out of his face, putting it behind his ear.

Waiting for him, her molecules slowed almost to a halt. Finally leaning in, they kissed, creating a whistling sound that could be heard throughout the Realm.

The cart stopped, and Kai helped Makani out and escorted her into her home. They were hand in hand, and when they arrived at Makani's door, they didn't want to let one another go. Holding Kai's face in her hands, she looked into his eyes, smiling. No words needed to be spoked between them. Kissing his lips gently, she released him and scurried into her room, almost slamming the door in his face. This had been a night to remember and she couldn't wait to write about the perfect first date, a date she would tell their many children about, in her diary so that she didn't forget a single detail.

Kai splashed excitedly back to the carriage, flowing euphorically, and filling the space with his bliss. The closer he got to home, the more he thought about his future. Yes, he may be preparing for a war soon, but he would also be preparing for the beauty that he knew would be his union to Makani.

Chapter Nine

Hell Hath No Fury

"Afi, Shanira is a danger to the Realm and all Elementals in it," Ava tried to reason with the Fire King.

"No, she's not!" he yelled, getting in her face.

"I will put you the hell out if you don't back down," Suavai promised calmly, rising from his seat.

"Don't worry, Suavai. Afi is all flame and no fire. He lets his soldiers do the dirty work for him," Ava insulted, not backing down and showing no fear. "This is a bad habit of yours, Afi. One that you've passed down to your daughter. She's hurt Lurra, and we know that she's the only one willing to tolerate her. If she'll turn on her, none of us are safe."

"Well, maybe it's time for the Fire Kingdom to take reign anyway," Afi said dismissively. Luga opened his mouth to speak, but Pa'u beat him to it.

"Nonsense," she spoke gently. She was nowhere near as vocal and flashy as her husband and daughter. But that meant that when she did speak, it was a serious matter. "Shanira doesn't deserve to rule even our kingdom. And she needs to learn that everything doesn't have to go her way. I've sat silently while you turned her into the selfish, entitled, spoiled being that she was. Your motivation hurt me more than your actions, seeking revenge for Suavai taking Ava from you. You refused to lose again. But what you've done, dear husband, is create a monster. And you should be the one to put the beast your created on a leash."

"I prefer not to be here," Matagi, the Wind King spoke up. Like their children, he and his wife Ea, like their children, hated being in the midst of unrest. They liked to keep things as light as possible. "But I will not subject my people to another war. Fix this!" he blasted, in a no-nonsense tone.

Everyone fell silent. Matagi's voicing his concerns, and with so much fervor showed the seriousness of the matter. Ea rubbed her husband's back in swirls, trying to calm him down. All eyes were on Pa'u and Afi. The reason for the First Realm War and the women going into hiding wasn't spoken aloud. It was known by all of the dignitaries, but to spare Pa'u any embarrassment, no one brought up her husband's secret love for another woman almost destroying everything that they all knew. Her speaking on it made it real, and the pain in her eyes was evident.

"All of them are worried about their children, their kingdoms, their people. Lurra has been harmed, and it could've been worse. Look around," she flashed a light in a crescent around the room, shining light on the faces of all in attendance at the secret meeting. "They are all honoring the treaty. A treaty you signed. If the Fire Kingdom was so great, we wouldn't have needed to sign that treaty. Your signature is an admission, if not in your heart, then in your head. You are the main one speaking of the danger of egos, but now, what are you doing? I do not desire our daughter being hurt, but if it is for the greater good, I'll destroy her myself."

Silence filled the room and Afi fell into his seat in concession. He knew what his wife spoke was truth, and although he had married her for convenience, he'd grown to love her. Seeing how his actions had harmed her, how embarrassed she was by the truth that she'd been forced to face her entire life, broke him. Looking around the room at the other faces, the faces of males and females that he'd once been friends with, Kings and Queens in their own right, and taking in their saddened expressions, he felt foolish. His eyes finally landing on Ava, the woman he'd loved so much that he couldn't fathom her being with another, his flames dimmed down to embers. His understanding was louder in his silence than it would've ever been if he'd said the words. Reaching over and taking Pa'u's hand, he kissed the back of it, feeling a spark that he'd never given the attention that it deserved.

"What do you need me to do?" he finally spoke, knowing that he may just be asked to do the unthinkable.

*****

Shanira and Lurra had witnessed the whole date. Once Kai and Makani had parted, Shanira burst into a flaming rage because she knew that she would not be Kai's choice for Queen. Lurra couldn't keep up as she blazed back to her Kingdom. So, instead of trying, she returned to the Water Kingdom.

"She's on a rampage," Lurra informed everyone when she was escorted into the chambers where the meeting was being held. All eyes were on her, and when they travelled down to her arm, she felt self-conscious.

"Where was she last?" Pa'u asked, sighing heavily.

"She was moving so fast that I didn't see—"

"She went home. To the Fire Kingdom," Kari gusted in advising them. When I left, she was convening the soldiers and threatening to have them punished for treason if they didn't obey her command.

Afi and Pa'u met eyes before blazing out of the room. Suavai put out the path that they left in their departure. When Afi and Pa'u arrived home, Shanira was gone. They sent some of the remaining soldiers, who were willing to die rather than assist Shanira, to find their daughter. When the soldiers returned empty-handed, everyone decided to call it a night and figured Shanira was somewhere sulking. It was quiet, so, although they all knew that something was brewing, everyone in the meeting, as well as Afi and Pa'u, decided to try to get some rest. But not before putting their armies on alert.

Exhausted from his date, Kai laid across his bed, awaiting his mother, Kari, and Lurra to come into his room and inform him of the state of things. He didn't know that he'd drifted off and was enjoying a reverie recap of his date with Makani, until he was awakened by a rumbling explosion that shook the walls of his entire Kingdom. His temperature began to rise as he realized that the explosion had hit the window to his room, the wooden walls blown open on fire. Before he could rise, Shanira was on top of him, steaming his being, weakening him.

"You chose that unstable, unreliable creature over me?" She raged. "I'll destroy you and your entire measly Kingdom. You're not fit to be a King anyway."

She wrapped him up in flames and blocked the door to his room with a burst of fire. While the Liquid Knights attempted to fight their way in, she dragged a now weakened Kai out of the window, where her band of flame thrower vigilantes were awaiting her command. She gave a nod and they began scorching the Water Kingdom's shields against the Orange Star's light. They went on to the Land Kingdom, burning everything they could.

They soon found that all of the Land and Water residences were vacant, as they had been sent to the Underground in expectation of an act such as this. A weakened Kai laughed at the defeated look that Shanira was unable to hide at this realization.

"I wouldn't laugh if I were you," Shanira stated, turning up her temperature, "they won't be any good without a King," she expressed her plan to destroy Kai.

"Shanira," Kari yelled, swirling around her, "release him!"

"No!" Shanira declared, "I will *not* be the laughing stock of the Realm because this imbecile doesn't know greatness when he sees it!"

She raised her temperature again, watching Kai evaporate into the air. Makani, while Shanira was distracted with Kari, morphed into a swirling whirlwind, snatching Shanira, her Flame Throwers, and Kai, into her center. Following Lurra's directions, she took the two of them to an airtight cave, on the far end of the Land Kingdom. As she swirled, Kai was able to lower his temperature and begin to restructure his molecules. Kari flew ahead to the cave to meet Lurra.

When they reached the cave, Makani flung Shanira and the Flame Throwers against its walls, disorienting them just long enough for Lurra to push the stone over its opening. Flying a few more feet ahead, she hovered over a nearby lake, sucking some of its water into her swirl until Kai was fully able to recompose himself.

Kari seeped into the cave, where Shanira was now raging, and sucked all of the air out of the enclosed space, turning her and her henchmen to embers and ash. With her parents' permission, Shanira was left there to smolder until the Council could decide what to do with her.

The three friends returned to the Water Kingdom, where the Fire soldiers were being deployed and instructed to rebuild everything that Shanira had destroyed. Kai rested in a Spring until he regained his strength. The Announcement Ceremony was the next day and he needed to recoup from the ordeal so that he could reveal his decision to the entire Realm. Makani never left his side. She stayed on the shore, moving the water to and from Kai all night.

Chapter Ten

The Perfect Pairing

The next day was a somber day to be one of celebration. Word of Shanira's actions had made it throughout the Realm and, though her attempts had been squelched, and she was in captivity, there was still fear and concern that this could lead to war. Knowing this, Afi took center stage, after all in the realm had been summoned. Showing a united front, the Kings and Queens of the Wind, Land, and Water Kingdoms all stood with him and his wife Pa'u, before the realm's occupants, as Afi gave a speech that he hoped would put all minds at ease.

"Although saddened by my daughter's actions, I wished to come before you all to inform you that she acted of her own fruition and her actions do not reflect the intentions of the Fire Kingdom. We have worked diligently to maintain peace within the realm. This has not changed. Though it is embarrassing, I feel that I am partly responsible. My heart was hardened, and I allowed my ego to feed hatred into the heart of my child. For that, I am sorry. This is a happy time for the Realm, as we will be inducting our first Realm King and Queen, as arranged in the treaty on this evening. This is a time for celebration and not fear. For many years, the Fire Kingdom has used fear to control not only its people, but all of you. We have learned from this, if nothing more, that humility, unity, and peace, are the only way for us to be successful as a whole and govern over Earth. This is the dawn of a new way for our realm. A new existence for all, and we all embrace it with open arms," Afi ended his speech, motioning for the other Kings and Queens to stand beside him.

The crowd burst into cheers and the fears were lifted. Leaving in waves, they all went to their respective homes to prepare for the Announcement Ceremony. It was almost a surety that Shanira wouldn't be Kai's choice, but everyone wanted to be present for the onset of this new age for the realm. The crowning of King Kai, and the announcement of his choice for mate and Queen of all elements. Most weren't sure what that would mean, but they were excited just the same.

*****

"I don't want to leave you," Makani whined to Kai, who was trying to convince her to head home to prepare for the evening's festivities.

"And that's why you're the female for me. But I promise, I'm fine. Now, go home, and get pretty for me," he flirted, kissing her lips gently.

"Fine. But if I get *one* report that you're not ok, Kai," she fussed.

"You're so sexy when you're mad," Kai teased, making Makani blush.

"Ewwww, save that for the honeymoon," Kari interrupted their tender moment, making Makani roll her eyes. He stepped out of one of the two carriages that had been sent by Ea and Matagi to pick up Makani and Kai.

"Who invited you?" Makani asked her brother, resting her hands on her puffy hips.

"Mommy and Pop, that's who," Kari said, matter-of-factly, sticking his tongue out at Makani playfully. "They sent me for you, and I'll make sure that cripple here gets home in one piece, so he can tell the whole realm how dope my big sis is."

Waving Kari off to not show him how much his words meant to her, Makani leaned down and kissed Kai one last time before walking to the carriage to be escorted home to prepare for the Ceremony where she would be the Woman of the Hour. The driver helped her into the carriage.

"Hey! Watch them hands," Kai yelled, teasingly but seriously as well, when the driver helped Makani inside of her carriage.

Makani looked back at Kai and Kari with a smile that spoke volumes, while the now rattled driver climbed up into his seat in the front of the carriage, giving Kai a respectful head nod before pulling away.

"Why you scare that man like that?" Kari asked, laughing.

"I just have to protect what's mine," Kai responded emphatically, in a tone that made Kari pull back with his hands raised in surrender.

Helping Kai up, it was evident that he'd regained a great deal of his strength. Neither of them wanted to take any chances, though, so with the help of the driver of the awaiting carriage. Kai poured himself into the carriage

"Say bruh," Kari got Kai's attention. "Thanks."

"For what?" Kai asked confused. He felt like he should've been the one thanking Kari for having his back through the entire process. "You're the one who lost your woman."

That made Kari laugh hysterically. Of all the things that he thought of Shanira, calling her his woman was the furthest thing from it. For him, she was a fling. A phenomenal fling, but not one worth losing everything over.

"She was far from my woman. But I'm thanking you for never doubting my loyalty."

"Neither one of us are virgins, man. I know what it's like when it's good to you. But you're a good dude. Always have been. I never doubted you for a second.

Nodding his head, Kari took Kai's words into account. With all the bad decisions that he'd made, Kai had never judged him. That was such a rare thing, especially when it came to their positions in the Realm. Being able to be himself set him up to see and embrace his greatness. He'd be forever grateful to Kai for that.

Kai meant what he'd said. Kari was his ace, and nothing or no one would ever come between them. He was glad to have Kari by his side even now, when he was headed to make the biggest decision of his life. The feelings of dread that once surrounded this ceremony were slowly leaving his mind the closer he got to his home. He had been able to find a way to honor the treaty, on his own terms, and he was proud of himself for that, and grateful to his parents for considering his life and the impact the treaty would have on it, before even he knew.

Feeling a shift in Kari's currents, Kai looked at him, awaiting for him to share his thoughts. Looking at Kai, his face balled up, Kari flipped into brother mode. Kai was his best friend, but he and Makani shared a womb. He needed to let him know that he wasn't going to be as loyal to his friend when it came to his sister.

"If you do her wrong, if you ever make her cry, I'll kill ya," Kari said in all seriousness.

"I gotcha man," Kai agreed, knowing that he had no intentions of doing anything but making Makani happy for the rest of their lives.

"Aight, now let's go crown you king!" Kari dapped Kai up and they both watched the scenery on their way to the Water Kingdom.

*****

Lurra was in her room, sadness filling her. She'd lost her best friend and love in Shanira, but the reality was settling in that she never had Shanira in her life in any capacity. She had been going through all the years that she'd been Shanira's fool and couldn't think of a single time when Shanira put her ahead of herself. Running a bristle into her hair, she tried to find a reason to be excited about the Ceremony she was preparing for.

"You look beautiful," Fauna came in and complimented her daughter. She'd been in a funk since they'd caged Shanira.

"Do you think she ever loved me?" Lurra asked her mother sadly.

"I do, my love. I just think she loved herself more, and that made her incapable of loving you properly," Fauna answered honestly. She knew that wasn't what Lurra may have wanted to hear, but it was the truth she needed to hear.

"I want to confront her, Mama! I want to tell her how badly she hurt me," Lurra wailed, Fauna patting the sap from her eyes before it could fall and destroy her almost perfect makeup.

"Then you should," she encouraged her daughter, who looked at her in shock. Of all the things that she expected her mother to say, that wasn't it. "If you think she'll care."

That dose of reality made Lurra smile, "That's more like it. I thought you'd lost your mind," she told her mother, laughing because she really did think she'd gone crazy.

"Get ready, the carriage arrives in twenty minutes," Fauna informed, leaving her daughter to make final preparations to leave, and going to make sure that her husband, who moved slower than molasses, was ready to go as well.

In her own thoughts, Lurra let the sap fall freely. She promised herself that these were the last tears that she would shed for Shanira, the woman she loved who taught her that love didn't always love you back.

*****

"Lovvvve is in the airrrrr," Matagi sang, sliding coyly into his daughter's room. He pulled her up from the chair that she was seated at in front of her vanity, spinning her around and around in a playful father-daughter slow dance.

"Pop, how did you know I was dressed?" Makani fussed, looking at her father lovingly. He was so light-hearted, even in his many millennia of presence, and that was the reason that she and Kari were so fun-loving.

"I knew you would waste no time getting ready for your big night. And Ea told me," Matagi admitted.

"She can't hold water," Makani fussed, shaking her head at her mother. She kept no secrets from her father, and that was the kind of relationship that Makani wanted for herself and Kai. She knew that his parents had a beautiful relationship, as well, and that gave her so much hope.

"No," Matagi laughed in gentle bursts. "But the question is... will *youuuu* be able to hold water? Because I need a lotta grands running around here now that I'm about to retire and hand the kingdom down to your brother."

Makani blushed, dissipating with embarrassment.

"No need to be embarrassed now," Ea came into the room looking around for Makani but only seeing Matagi and feeling their daughter's shamed presence. "How do you think you got here?"

"Ewwww, y'all nasty," Makani teased, finally regaining shape as her parents kissed one another passionately. "Can y'all take that to your lair? I don't want to see all that. And while you're talking to me about children, it looks like y'all are about to be making some more when that empty nest syndrome kicks in."

"Now that's funny," Matagi surged with laughter. "After you and your brother, we're good on children of our own. Trust me," he said, quite seriously.

"Doesn't mean we can't practice," Ea added, sauntering out of the room with Matagi on her heels.

"Don't make me late being nasty," Makani yelled at her parents who exited her room playing a cat and mouse game. "They're gonna make me late," she laughed, shaking her head and putting the finishing touches on her makeup.

Wearing a Harpy Couture original, her all-white gown consisted of a cumulus corset bodice with flowing wispy breeze airstream skirt flowing in layers to her ankles. She wore Stiletto Sky's peep-toed pumps. Checking herself in the full-length mirror, she admired the silver starburst eye shadow and twilight pouty pink lip tint on her lips.

Leaving her room, she chose not to see what her parents were up to, for fear of being traumatized. Instead, she made her way to the carriage, planning to send it back around for her parents, hoping that their activities didn't cause them to miss the entire ceremony. Accepting the hand of the tuxedo-clad driver and sitting nervously in the cushioned seats on her way to the Water Kingdom. It was the final day of Serah, and the day that she would assume the throne of the realm with Kai.

*****

"I couldn't be prouder of you," Suavai entered the room complimenting his son. He meant every word of it.

He and Kai hadn't always seen eye-to-eye, but he knew it was because of how similar they were. Placing his hand on his son's shoulder, he felt the nervousness shifting beneath his poised surface. Even the jellyfish that he had floating around inside his form were being tossed from left to right.

"When you married mama, how did you shake the unrest that flowed through you?" Kai asked his father for advice. It wasn't that he didn't want to be paired with Makani, but the fear of failing as her mate had him in an unrestful state.

"With a big cloak and a lot of seafoam to camouflage it," Suavai admitted to his son with a laugh. "Don't feel bad because you're nervous. If you weren't nervous, I would be concerned.

"Do the flutters ever stop when you see her walk into a room?" Kai asked. He and Suavai had never had the love conversation. It was both their assumptions that the union would be political and not one of passion.

Looking behind himself hearing Ava step into the doorway, Suavai smiled and Kai got his answer when his father's tide shifted almost as powerfully as his own was.

"You look so handsome," Ava mused, looking at Kai. "And you clean up pretty well, too, old man," she grinned at Suavai.

Kai admired their love like he had so many times in his life. And now, the idea of having that for himself excited him even more. He chose not to hide his feelings. He wanted Makani to see how she made him feel. She deserved to see that he felt as strongly for her as she did for him.

"You ready?" Suavai asked his son, proudly. His chest poked out and he was happy to see his son's demeanor matching his. He hadn't taken his eyes off of his wife, the woman that had been by his side, even when she could have lost her life and felt as much love for her as he had the first day he laid eyes on her.

"Let's do this," Kai replied, both men stepping to either side of Ava and taking one of her arms in each of theirs.

"Awwww, my boys," Ava bubbled before her joy overflowed, floating into the air. She had the two most handsome males in the realm accompanying her into the Announcement Ceremony. She'd never felt so majestic.

*****

The night of the Announcement Ceremony, the uneasiness filled the ballroom. No one danced. No one ate. Everyone was on edge. They shifted in their seats uneasily as the Royalty descended the steps to take their seats. Kai wanted to ease the minds of the people, *his people*, so he wasted no time with the formalities. As soon as everyone was seated, he stood, his anemone crown sitting comfortably upon his head and seaweed cape hanging from his broad shoulders. He had filled himself with sharks and sting rays as a depiction of his power.

"My people," he began, "there will be no war. Through the efforts of all Kingdoms working together, what could have been a detrimental act at the hands of an angry being was thwarted. I am proud of our efforts and the fact that they saved many lives. With the assistance of the present Royalty, my chosen Queen, the Wind Princess Makani and Chief Councilors, Prince Kari and Princess Lurra, proved our ability to unite for the sake of the Realm. We have every intention of continuing to do so."

Kai paused, looking at his friends, and future Queen lovingly.

"On this night of celebration, let us not allow the fear and terror that Shanira wished to impart upon us to consume us. I have found my Queen, honored the Treaty, and, with the assistance of her and my Council, under the guidance of the standing Royalty, we will live this Serah, and every subsequent one, in peace," Kai concluded.

The ballroom erupted into a roar of applause. The mood lightened, and the Whale Orchestra played, as the soon-to-be Realm King and Queen, Kai and Makani, danced alongside their people, celebrating the dawn of a new era in the Realm.

The End

About the Author

Joi Miner, 38, is a mother of two beautiful daughters from Montgomery, AL (currently residing in Birmingham, AL). She is a full-time author, editor, performance poet, storyteller, sexual assault and domestic violence activist, and entrepreneur, who loves spending time with her family, hosting shows, and listening to good music. She enjoys writing engaging stories, with plot twists that keep readers on their seats! As a freelance non-fiction contributor, for her personal blog, as well as well-known blog sites such as Negus Who Read and I Am The F-Bomb, she shares her insights into this crazy world we live in.

I'd Love to Hear from You!

Here's how to find me:

[My Blog] My Life Is A Joi Miner Novel: www.mylifeisajoiminernovel.com

Email: authorjoiminer@gmail.com

Twitter: @joiminer

Instagram: joiminer

Facebook: https://www.facebook.com/joiminer

Facebook Overflow Profile: https://www.facebook.com/authorjoiminer

Author Page: https://www.facebook.com/joiminer2

Subscribe to my Newsletter: http://eepurl.com/cKJ7bf